THE BLUERIDGE JUNCTION BOYS

BOUND TO FIGHT

CODY AND KENNEDY

A.D. ELLIS

WWW.FACEBOOK.COM/ADELLISAUTHOR

COPYRIGHT © 2018

COVER, SPINE, BACK BY

KAY SIMONE

AT

KAY SIMONE CREATIVE

QUOTES OF INSPIRATION

"Love is the only force capable of transforming an enemy into a friend."

~Martin Luther King, Jr.

"From the deepest desires often come the deadliest hate."

~Socrates

"Hatreds are the cinders of affection."

~Sir Walter Raleigh

DEDICATION

To Kurt and Chris for their openness and assistance
in getting this story told.

INTRODUCTION

I fell in love with the male/male romance genre back when I wrote my first one (<u>Sawyer, Torey Hope: The Later Years</u>) and couldn't wait to write the six books in my male/male romance series <u>Something About Him</u>. As the most recent series was coming to an end, I started to wonder just what I would write next.

I grew up in small farming community with a railroad running only about 4 houses down from where I lived, so small towns and railroads are familiar to me. My mind started playing with the idea of these three men (Micah, his cousin Levi, and their best friend Cody) growing up on a hill in this small railroad town. *Blueridge* was the name that came to me. Well, then my head started playing with words and landed on nicknaming the series The BJ Boys, so I created Blueridge Junction and the rest is history.

These three stories combine some of my very favorite male/male romance tropes.

In Micah and Cole's story (<u>Fight For It</u>) we find a mechanic and a teacher in an out-for-you tale.

<u>Can't Fight It</u> is a story of opposites attract and May/December romance.

<u>Bound to Fight</u> combines the best of leather daddies and enemies-to-lovers for a great story.

CAST OF CHARACTERS

Micah Edwards- Mechanic in Blueridge Junction, cousin of Levi, best friend of Cody.

Cole Pierce- Teacher at the high school

Levi Wells- Tattoo artist in Blueridge Junction, cousin of Micah, best friend of Cody

Jay Owens- Dancer at Strip Teaze, much younger than the rest of the guys

Cody Parker- Manages his family-owned restaurant/bar (BJ's Burgers & Beer or the B & B) Friends with Levi and Micah

Kennedy Marks- Local police officer in Blueridge Junction

CHAPTER 1

CODY PARKER

A sharp crack of a whip snapped through the air courtesy of the BDSM demonstration taking place in the middle of the room. The show began with a flogger presentation and would end with a display of several different cock rings, ball gags, and nipple clamps. I prided myself on bringing both entertaining and educational events for the men who frequented the B & B.

The B & B, as the locals called it, had been in my family for longer than I'd been alive. BJ's Burgers & Beer was a pillar in the town of Blueridge Junction just as the founding families were. The Parker, Edwards, and Wells names were part of BJ's history.

Living in a small town such as Blueridge Junction meant no sex shops were nearby. From the very tame to more extreme kink, the B & B provided gay men into the leather scene with a full array of demos and the chance to act out their kinks and fantasies in a safe and open environment. While actual sex in the bar was frowned upon, many men came to learn, to be entertained, and to find the next object of their desire. Pairs looking to add a third or a fourth to their play, couples searching for a polyamorous setup, men prowling for a hookup, and men who just enjoyed the connection and camaraderie they found within the leather scene could often be found at B&B's Leather Sundays.

"Good turn out." Kennedy Marks leaned on the bar, his built, yet slim body framed by the stained glass windows running the length of the wall.

My gut immediately churned with a mixture of anger and desire. There was no specific reason why I despised Kennedy, I just did. We were both very strong, confident, assertive men. Maybe that was why he constantly rubbed me the wrong way. But, damn the man was fucking sexy as hell.

"Yeah, looks like everyone is enjoying themselves." I gave a curt nod as the scent of food, beer, leather, and men drifted through the air.

"You got some young sub in mind for later?" Kennedy smirked.

My broad frame, dark looks, and dominant personality in my day-to-day life automatically gave way to people assuming I was a dominant in the bedroom. I didn't deny the assumption.

"Yeah, I've seen a couple guys who may fit the bill." In truth, I'd seen quite a few young sub boys looking for a daddy and I knew I'd have no problem getting them into bed. But, those young men desperately searching for a dom weren't what had truly caught my eye.

"Sounds promising." Kennedy waggled his brow. "I've been checking that guy out." He jerked his chin toward a beefy man across the room.

"Looks like just your type."

"Definitely." Kennedy nodded in agreement.

Kennedy and I usually had two types of conversation. The first when we argued about absolutely anything and everything. The second when we awkwardly tried to make small talk.

My best friend Micah and his partner, Cole, wandered up to the bar.

The couple weren't deep into the leather scene, but they enjoyed learning about new products and meeting other gay men so they frequented Sundays at the B & B quite often.

On a regular weekday, the locals would be grabbing food in the restaurant section, chatting with friends or associates, or enjoying a beer at the bar. But, it wasn't a regular weekday.

It was a Sunday.

Sundays weren't exclusive or by invite only, but patrons *not* involved in the leather scene were expected to understand that the B & B would be catering to gay men. From very casual jeans and t-shirts with leather boots to the more intricate leather chaps, vests, and leather sir caps, a person could always find a wide variety on Sundays. During special events, the bar was filled with a lot more bare skin thanks to harnesses and jock straps.

I'd had a lot of work cut out for me to get Sunday afternoons in a small Midwest town set up as a location hosting the gay leather scene, but I'd made it work. Some backlash occurred when I first started, but most locals either enjoyed coming in to feed their curiosities, support a friend or family member, or they chose to ignore Sundays at the B & B all together. It helped that I was a member of the founding families and one of the town's favorite sons.

"What do you all think of the product demonstration?" I broke from my reverie.

"*Very* interesting." Micah grinned and pulled Cole close to his side. "I think we may be making some purchases."

"You guys got room for a sling in your house?" Kennedy teased.

Cole blushed. "Pretty sure we're not ready for a sling yet."

"But the cock rings have become quite a favorite." Micah kissed the top of Cole's head.

"I'm going to see if I can find a piece of ass before heading out." Kennedy slapped Micah on the back. "I've got a string of shifts coming up at the department, I better enjoy while I can."

The three of us watched Kennedy walk away. I fought off the image of him in his police uniform wielding his baton and cuffs.

"When are you two going to finally give in and admit you're hot for each other?" Micah's words were light, but I bristled.

"That's bullshit. Two men like Kennedy and me are bound to fight. We don't get along at all. Barely able to have a conversation for longer than five minutes before we're disagreeing about something." I shook my head. "You sound just like Levi and Jay." My other best friend, Jay and his partner also had crazy ideas that Kennedy and I should be together.

"The air positively crackles with sexual tension any time you two are around each other," Cole threw in his two cents.

"Well, you all can see what you want to see, but Kennedy and I are *not* a good match. Period." I grabbed a rag from behind the bar and started to wipe down an already sparkling bar top.

"Yeah, that fiery glare you've got locked on Kennedy right now totally proves there's nothing there." Micah rolled his eyes and took Cole's hand.

Realizing too late that my eyes had betrayed me, I tried to break the gaze to no avail. I watched Kennedy's tall, slim body press up against the big, broad, muscular man he'd indicated earlier. The man grabbed his elbow and led Kennedy toward the door.

"Damn, looks like you lost your chance." Micah nudged me.

"Shut it. Just give it up," I growled.

Micah and Cole laughed as they walked away. "See ya, big guy. Hope you find what you're looking for tonight." Micah threw an arm up in a goodbye.

Pushing Kennedy far, far to the back of my mind, I stayed through the end of the product demo and began to clean up. Monday morning the B & B would be completely back to a normal with only those who'd visited on Sundays any the wiser.

"You got plans for later?" A young man, likely in his mid to late twenties, eyed me from the bar as he tongued the straw in his fruity cocktail.

"Depends." I fought to control my eye roll. I knew the routine. He'd flirt and suggest a hookup in not so many words. I'd take him somewhere, boss him around, give him the fucking he so obviously wanted, and we'd call it a night. I hadn't seen him around before, but they were all the same. All so much the fucking same. Sex was sex, so why was I feeling so irritated and bored and out of sorts with the regular routine lately?

When the boy slurped his empty drink, I caught his gaze. "What are you drinking?"

"Sex on the Beach, but I'd settle for sex with the bartender." He bit his bottom lip and perched his tight little ass on the edge of his stool.

Making quick work of the cocktail, I slid the concoction toward him. *Yes, I was purposely being an obtuse ass.*

"Um, thanks?" Little Boy quirked his brow before sipping the drink. "What's this for?"

"You said you wanted Sex with the Bartender." I gestured toward the glass in his hand.

He blushed. "Oh, um, I didn't realize it was the name of a drink."

I chuckled. "I know."

He watched my every move as I finished cleaning up. Deciding I'd put him out of his misery, I took his empty glass before gripping his shoulder. "I don't do hookups at my place. You live close?"

"About an hour away," the boy hesitated, "but I've got a car."

Feeling proud and impressed that my Sundays at the B & B had drawn the kid from an hour away, I shoved down the disgruntled part that wanted to complain about sex in a car at the age of "thirty-ish". I'd never taken anyone to my house, because it never felt right. But, a fuck in the backseat of a car made me feel like I was back in high school. Looking the kid over, knowing he'd never have gotten past my bouncers without a legal identification card, I figured he was horny enough that we'd be in and out of his car within the hour. I glanced at my watch. I'd be home in time for a shower and the late news. "Let's go then." I reached out and gave him a little shove toward the door.

The kid's eyes lit up before he sauntered slowly toward the exit.

"Come on, kid, I don't need this to take all night." I grumbled as I locked up.

"You going to punish me if I'm a bad boy?" He stuck a finger in his mouth and bit down.

Gah, playing the dom used to give me such a rush, but these days it felt like a routine, a script, or a scene to be played out. Maybe I was looking for something kinkier? *Maybe you want to reverse the roles?* Hell, no. I'd never met anyone I would voluntarily submit to. The dom role may have left me feeling a little unfulfilled from time to time, but submitting control to a man wasn't something I was looking for either.

Was it?

"Yeah, I'll spank your ass red if you don't hurry up." I pushed him again and he led me to his car.

Fifteen minutes later, I'd given him the expected spanking and shoved my dick down his throat until he gagged. Foreplay over, I rolled a condom down my length while he panted under me. Face down, ass up, his pretty pink hole waited for me. "You ready to take me like the little bitch you are?"

"Give it to me. Give me that monster cock, daddy." The kid seemed to be into it if his heavy breathing, moaning, and squirming were any indication.

His words didn't do much for me. But my dick was an equal opportunity fucker so I slid deep inside his tight pucker. Dom and sub, Daddy and son, kinky or vanilla, my cock wasn't turning down the chance to get milked by a sweet little ass.

Your ass probably wouldn't turn down the chance to milk a big ol' cock while it pounded deep inside you either.

As the thought hit me hard, I groaned as Kennedy's face appeared in my mind as well as a vision of him pounding my ass. "Oh fuck," Where the hell had *that* thought come from?

"Yeah, baby, give it to me," the kid chanted under me.

Reaching around to jack his dick before I shot my load, I assured myself that the image of Kennedy was a complete and total fluke.

But, after I'd finished, cleaned up, and left the kid's car, I was hit with the sinking realization that random hookups with men who only wanted to be under me weren't what I wanted anymore. But, what did that mean for someone with the reputation of being a top?

And what the hell was I doing thinking about Kennedy Marks so much?

CHAPTER 2

KENNEDY MARKS

I woke up stiff and sore from the kinky shit Beefy Daddy put me through the night before. God, I hated myself every single morning after. I had known I was different from about middle school on, but hadn't actually figured out I was gay until much later. After a broken engagement with a woman, I finally gave my difference a name. Letting dominant men push me around and control me in bed was something I fell into easily after the nightmare I called my childhood. It wasn't what I truly wanted, but it was all my head told me I was good for. Aside from my police officer job, I was weak and worthless in all other aspects of life.

At least that's what had been beaten into my head from birth until age ten.

And it's what I believed. Even though I hid it well.

Stumbling from bed, I headed for the kitchen while congratulating myself that I'd had the sense to come home and shower before crashing. My one-bedroom garden apartment was only a block away from the police station. I set the coffee pot to brew and measured out some steel cut oats and water in a pot. The oats would be almost ready by the time I finished my shower.

Once in the bathroom, I turned the water on as hot as I could stand it. As the room filled with steam, my mind filled with unwanted images of last night. Sex was enjoyable, but being manhandled and bossed around while tied up wasn't what I wanted the most. In the beginning, when I was figuring out my sexuality and venturing into the world of hookups and dates, I found it somewhat exciting that dominant men found me attractive and wanted me. The fact that they used me and abused me seemed to fit with the way I'd been raised, so I let it happen. But over the years, a seed had taken root deep inside my heart and mind. That seed had sprouted and told me that I wanted to be the one in control. *I* wanted to take a man the way I'd been taken. *I* wanted to put him through pain to find pleasure.

My common sense would quickly shoot down that idea each and every time. No man would look at me and want me to dominate him. I was fairly attractive in a very normal way. I kept in shape by running so I had a nice build even if I was on the lean side. But I wasn't a large man, at six foot and two hundred pounds nothing about me screamed, *I'd top you so hard.* Even though that's exactly what my heart and mind wanted.

In reality, I wouldn't have enjoyed topping Beefy Daddy. All of my weaknesses and insecurities would have rushed to the surface. However, fantasies of having the right man under me, bringing him to the brink of pleasure over and over again, and pushing his body to the very limit with mutually desired tools of pain, well…those thoughts haunted me as much as the horrific memories of my childhood. But what man would want *me* to strap him to a sling or flog his skin red or tease his clamped nipples?

As the hot water rained down, I leaned an arm against the tile and then completely uninvited images of Cody Parker filled my mind. Cody was as top as they came and, while I wouldn't pass up a chance to have sex with him, we were more likely bound to get into a knockdown drag out fight than to end up in bed together. Cody and I had no specific beef; we just rubbed each other the wrong way.

Correction.

I rubbed Cody the wrong way.

He was simply a minor annoyance. I let him take the lead in the whole, *we hate each other* thing. If he wanted to hate me, I was used to that and could deal.

But I couldn't deal with the pictures playing through my head, causing my cock to grow hard in my hand. Cody on his hands and knees, a ball gag in his mouth, a leather harness connected to a ring clamped tightly around his cock and balls, and a bright red patch of skin where my hand had left its mark on his perfectly tight ass.

As the bedroom scene played out in my mind, I groaned in the foggy bathroom as I stroked my dick. Cody's bubble butt was on display, his pretty pink hole pulsing, almost daring me to slide in my cock. I pulled the harness to bring Cody to his knees, his ear right at my mouth as his back pressed tightly against my chest.

"You've got a beautiful ass, Parker. An ass that looks amazing with my mark on it," I whispered in his ear as Cody shivered and moaned. "I'm thinking it may look even better with my long, hard cock stretching and filling you. What do you think?"

Cody whimpered.

I shoved him to the bed and groaned in anticipation as his ass spread open for me. After another hard smack to his smooth skin, I rubbed a soothing hand over the intended sting before moving down to feast upon him.

I'd been rimmed. I'd done the rimming. But never with a man completely and totally under my control. I swirled and teased my tongue over his hole before dipping inside.

The thought brought me abruptly out of my reverie and I slammed my fist against the shower wall. "Stupid. Cody Parker is the last guy on the face of this damn earth who would bend over for you." Yet I as already too far into the fantasy so, I pumped my cock and imagined what it would be like to breach Cody's tight hole with my steely length. Once I came all over my fist, I watched the dream disappear as quickly as my jizz slid down the drain.

Pushing the scene to the furthest recesses of my mind, I dried, dressed, and attempted to shake off the feeling of disgust that filled me.

You're weak.

You're a joke.

You're worthless.

You couldn't control the past, and you still can't take charge and be a real man.

The words tumbled through my head on repeat, and my heart ached while my stomach soured.

I went through the motions of pouring my coffee and spooning my oats into a bowl. Breakfast went down easily though I tasted none of it as I wallowed in insecurities from my past brought to light by my insane fantasy in the shower.

My phone's buzz offered something other than self-loathing to think about.

Jay's name pop up on the screen.

"Hello?"

"Hey, Officer Kinky Pants. I'm outside. Let me in." Jay's voice was much too chipper for the way I was feeling, but I knew trying to turn him away was pointless. Jay always found a way to get what he wanted. It had taken him more than two years to finally land Levi Wells, but Jay had been persistent and never let Levi's reluctance deter him. Now they were happy in love and proving that opposites *do* attract and age was just a meaningless number.

I took one last sip of coffee before walking to the door and opening it.

Jay Owens stood there in all his glory. Sparkly lipstick, glitter eyeshadow, lashes any woman would die for, and his brown hair styled purposely messy, flopping just right over his forehead. Only Jay could pull off a pink tank, black sweatpant capris, and tall rainbow socks with black hi-tops.

"Nice outfit," I murmured in lieu of a hello.

"Right? I'm heading to teach a dance class at the high school. Figured I'd dress to impress." Jay sashayed himself right in and headed toward the kitchen. "I smell coffee. Please tell me you have either tons of sugar and creamer or you can make me some tea. I need caffeine." Jay hopped up on the countertop. "Eeew, is that oatmeal?"

"Yeah, want some?" I pulled a tea bag from the pantry and put a mug of water in the microwave.

"No, no, no. Me and oatmeal have a bad relationship." Jay wrinkled his nose. "Do you have any cereal?"

Knowing Jay would eventually get to the reason for his early morning call, I opened the pantry for him to see the selection of cereals I had in sealed plastic containers. Things always went stale way too quickly when left in the box. "Take your pick."

Jay hopped from the counter and sauntered to the pantry. "You wound me." His hand grasped at his chest in mock astonishment.

I cocked my brow.

"You ask a Queen to pick a cereal as if you don't already know which I'm going to choose." Jay propped a fist on his hip.

"What cereal do you want?" I wasn't in the mood for Jay's theatrics.

"Um, duh. *Fruity* Pebbles? I mean, that's like the gay man's cereal, is it not?" Jay chuckled at his own joke before grabbing the container and going to the cabinet for a bowl. "I mean, at least the choice was easy. I would have been in a tither deciding between Fruity Pebbles and Honey Smacks. 'Oh *honey*, you can *smack* my ass any time.'" He laughed again and poured the colorful pieces into his bowl.

"Don't leave it on the counter." I sat back down to await Jay's reason for being at my house.

"Of course not, I'd never leave a mess on your countertops." Jay replaced the container in the pantry and grabbed the milk from the fridge.

"No, just on your own countertops." I smirked at the story Levi had told me recently about Jay's crafting experience.

"Hey, that wasn't on purpose!" Jay took a large bite of his breakfast. "Mmmm, I love crisp cereal. God how I hated when the cereal would get stale at home." Jay seemed lost in thought for a moment. I knew he'd had a rough childhood, as well. He didn't know about mine. Appearing to break from his memories, Jay shrugged. "Who knew that tie-dye was better done outside?" Jay huffed at my raised brow. "Okay, okay. But it was raining and gross outside and I wanted to do the project right then." He took another bite. "I mean, I got it cleaned up."

"After almost giving Levi a heart attack. He told me he thought a unicorn had bled out in his kitchen." I laughed. "You have to be careful with him. His ticker is a lot older than yours, he can't handle surprises the way you can."

Jay pouted. "First, don't ever let *him* hear you say that. Second, he's not *that* much older. And I'm getting him used to coming home and being surprised. *Expect the unexpected* is our theme."

We sat in silence while Jay finished his Fruity Pebbles and tea.

I started my third cup of coffee. "So," I hedged.

Jay glanced up. "Oh right. You're probably wondering why I'm here and not cuddled up in bed with my Daddy showing him some morning loving."

"You could have stopped without the visual."

"Where's the fun in that?" Jay winked. "So, I need your help at The Blue Jay."

The Blue Jay was a new community center type project that Jay and Levi were starting. The BJ, once up and running, was the way Jay planned to help kids who were struggling as he did as a child. According to Jay's ideal plan, the center would be opened and staffed twenty-four seven to provide dance, art, and music classes along with counseling, tutoring, and mentoring.

When Jay had told our little group of his plans for The Blue Jay, he'd said, "The money from my mom was mine to begin with. I want to use it to help in some way. If I'd had a place like The Blue Jay to go when I was younger or a place to escape the bad and focus on the good then maybe things wouldn't have sucked so much. My goal is to make things a little easier on kids who are having a rough time." Jay had blushed and smiled sadly. "I recognize the irony in the whole situation. My mom is the reason my childhood sucked. But, my mom is also the reason I'm able to provide assistance to other kids. So, in a way, my mom caused my suffering and allowed my dream to come true at the same time. That's sort of a mind fuck."

Jay finished his cereal and carried the bowl to the sink.

"Just rinse the bowl and put it in the dishwasher, I need to run a cycle anyway." I joined him at the sink and rinsed my coffee cup.

Jay grabbed his sugar mixed with a little tea and gracefully danced himself en pointe to sit at the table. "So, like I said, The Blue Jay. We have some of the plans worked out and even some of the people worked out. But we need to get the word out, raise some funds, remodel the building, and plan a grand opening."

"Okay," I drew the word out not sure what Jay was wanting from me.

"I need my BJ Boys to help with all of that." Jay gestured with his hand as if swishing the request toward me.

"Um, okay. I'll help with whatever you need." I had no issues helping as I believed The Blue Jay would be a great place.

"We're meeting at Levi's place Friday night to create, plan, discuss, and be awesome. Can you be there?" Jay's words held hope, and I felt relieved I wasn't going to let him down.

"You're in luck. I have the whole weekend off, because I worked three extra shifts last week." I had wondered what I'd do with my time off. Now I knew I'd be with some of the best guys in BJ helping to do something good. Something that maybe could have helped me when I was young. Or would I have been too scared, weak, and stupid to figure out a place like The Blue Jay even existed?

"Yay!"

Jay's vivacious clapping pulled me from my haunted self-loathing.

"Can you come over around three on Friday?"

"Whoa, we need that much time to get this worked out?" I shrugged. "Sure, I can be there. We gonna order food?"

"Yeah, we'll have something delivered or go pick up something. Maybe Cody can even bring something from the B & B." Jay checked his phone. "Let's plan a big ol' fashioned sleepover! We haven't done that since my birthday. Yes! That's a great idea. I'll let the other guys know. Three on Friday so, pack a bag. Bring your sexy undies…" His eyes went wide and he snapped his fingers. "Oh, you *could* bring the ones I got you."

I rolled my eyes. Jay had gotten the whole group underwear as gifts back when it was *his* birthday. And, of course, Jay had gone overboard with the sexiness of the underwear. "I seriously don't think I'll ever have a need to wear those."

Jay pouted for a moment before shrugging and waving his arm in a flourish. "Okay, I've need to head out. Duty calls. I've got to go teach these teenagers how to be fabulous. It's a hard and thankless job, but somebody has to do it." Jay kissed my cheek, stuck his tea cup in the dishwasher, and sashayed himself right through the living room and out the front door before I'd even realized what happened.

I sat in stunned silence as my mind adjusted to the whirlwind that was Jay. He was like the Tasmanian devil. More graceful maybe, but still a ball of constant motion. I shook my head and stood up. Grabbing my bag, phone, and keys, I headed out the door to the station. I was on a three-day string of weird ass shifts that would fuck up my sleep and mess with my mind. But, police work was one of the only things I was truly *good* at, so I put one hundred percent effort into my job while there. And now, thanks to Jay, I'd have time to rest and relax with friends over the weekend.

CHAPTER 3

CODY

I parked my truck at Levi's on Friday and headed up the front steps. The property had once belonged to his parents, but they were killed in a car wreck when we were seniors in high school, and the land had been turned over to Levi. He managed the main house, guesthouse and land with the skill of a seasoned property owner from the age of eighteen. The Wells homestead sat on Blueridge Hill, smack dab between the Edwards' places, my family's homestead. All three properties had been built with servants' quarters, which were later turned into guest homes. Levi had eventually moved into the main house. Micah and Cole lived in Levi's guesthouse for a while, but they were married now and had built a home just up the hill. I moved from my parents' basement to the guest house at age eighteen and my sister, Sadie, eventually took over the basement at my parents'.

The layout of homes on Blueridge Hill never ceased to amaze me. The hill itself was co-owned by the Edwards, Wells, and Parker families back at least two generations allowing for only our families to build and live on the hill.

Chuckling at my mind's impromptu history review I knocked on the door as I realized I didn't see Levi's truck. I checked my phone. Three o'clock just like Jay had requested. Where was Levi?

Jay's smiling face appeared as he yanked open the door and pulled me inside. "I'm so glad you're here! Don't ever forget that I absolutely *adore* you."

"Um, okay?" I cocked a brow and studied the man-child I'd grown to care about. Jay's cheeks were flushed, his eyes perfectly outlined, and his lips stained a deep purple. "You look hyped about something. What's up?"

Jay waved me off. "Just excited about getting The Blue Jay running and having my best friends help."

"So, where's Levi? I thought he'd be here." I grabbed a cold bottle of water from the fridge.

"He's on his way, had to finish at the shop." Jay grabbed a full wine glass and took a sip.

"Drinking at three in the afternoon on a Friday?"

Jay winked. "It's five o'clock somewhere."

"Are Micah and Cole coming too?" I found myself looking forward to this impromptu get together as the week came to an end. I needed to be back at the B & B for an hour or two on Saturday and for the weekly leather gathering at three on Sunday, but aside from that, I had the whole weekend to hang with the guys.

"Yeah, a little later. Cole had some stuff to catch up on at school, and Micah had two more oil changes to finish before they both went home to shower, pack, and come over." Jay drained his glass. "Hey, can I borrow your phone?"

I reached for my phone in my back pocket. "Shit, I left it in the truck with my bag. I can get it."

"No, don't worry. You can get it later." Jay rushed from the room. "I'll just grab mine!" he yelled from the back of the house. When he came back to the kitchen, he grinned at a knock on the door. "Oh! Head on down to the basement. We're doing the planning down there. Levi doesn't want the main level messed up with my need to spread out and create."

I laughed. That sounded just like Levi and Jay. I made it exactly six steps down before nostalgia overtook me.

Micah, Levi, and I had thought we were awesome hanging out in the basement as pre-teens. After the Wells were killed and the three of us took to spending more time together mostly Micah and I wanting to keep an eye on Levi—we thought we were hot shit as teens hanging out in this basement.

We'd turned it into an absolute man cave haven with a full-sized refrigerator, huge television, and three gaming systems along with a fabulous sound system and computer work stations. We'd rested, relaxed, gamed, worked, and grew closer than we'd ever been before. Sure, gay porn and some random blow jobs had taken place down there, as well, but those instances just added to the fond memories.

Levi had added a lot to the basement since we were kids. He'd remodeled it to have a fully functional kitchenette, bathroom, and bedroom of sorts just off the main room. It reminded me of a studio apartment, but was actually probably a lot nicer. I'd urged Levi to rent out at least his guesthouse if not his basement for several years, but he'd always balked saying he enjoyed his privacy too much.

"So, we're meeting down here to get the plans all hatched, laid out, and ready to execute." Jay spoke as he came down the stairs.

The tramping feet and legs that appeared behind him were a swift kick to the gut and lit my fuse quicker than a match to gasoline.

"Why did you ask *him* to come?" My anger increased when I realized what a whiny-ass brat I sounded like.

"Nice to see you too, Parker." Kennedy's sarcasm was evident as he descended the last step.

"Now, Cody, be nice. Kennedy is my friend just as much as he is yours and the rest of the guys." Jay pointed a finger at me. Standing between Kennedy and I, he pressed a hand against both our chests, his arms stretched out like a T. "Damn, what I wouldn't give to be the filling of *this* sandwich," Jay mused. "But, I digress. You boys be good and please try to get along for me."

"I can if you can." Kennedy glanced my way.

"Whatever." I shrugged.

"I need to use your phone to order the food." Jay held out his hand to Kennedy.

"I thought you were getting your phone?" My mood had taken a turn for the worse.

Jay popped a hip and cocked his elbow out. "Dead battery. Do you want food or not?"

I waved him off and wandered to the couch. After flopping down onto the soft brown suede cushions, I ran both hands over my face. No matter how hard I tried to ignore Kennedy and the thoughts of him that were pounding to be let loose in my head, I couldn't do it. The image of Kennedy's face appearing in my mind while I fucked some nameless guy came rushing in and caused my head to pound. No amount of rubbing my temples could ease the extreme anger and confusion of those images.

"Damn, signal is bad down here. I'm going upstairs to call. You boys play nice while I'm gone." Jay pointed a warning finger our way.

Once he left, I squirmed as an awkward silence descended.

"So..." Kennedy sat in the recliner.

"So, what?" I snapped.

"Fuck, man. I get it, you hate me, but cut the asshole behavior," Kennedy groused.

"Yeah, well, it seems to come naturally, but I'll attempt to control it at least for the weekend." I was planning how to kill and dismember Jay's body. There were many hiding places for body parts all over the hill. He'd never be found.

Kidding. Of course, I was kidding.

"He's a good kid, and I'm excited for The Blue Jay to get up and running. I think it will be great for the young people in town and even some of the surrounding towns." Kennedy appeared to be steering the conversation to something we could both agree on.

"Yeah, it will be good." I nodded. "May face a little opposition at first, and take a little while to get word out about the place, but I think Jay will draw troubled kids in like the damned Pied Piper."

"Can't face any more opposition than you did in setting up the leather Sundays, right?" Kennedy cocked a brow.

"No way. The Blue Jay is for troubled youth, not many people are going to resist helping kids in need." I smirked. "Kinky leather daddies and their boys are a *whole* different story."

"I have to say I'm really surprised the town has accepted or chosen to ignore the B & B turning leather every Sunday afternoon," Kennedy mused. "BJ isn't the most liberal of towns and the Midwest isn't known for being accepting of differences or change or kink."

"Yeah, I'm likely on a one-way path straight to Hell according to some of the town folk. But, it's amazing how accepting people become, or at least how willing they are to turn a blind eye, when they get wind of *who* is attending leather Sundays. Friend and family loyalty runs deep in BJ. Residents may not *love* the mysterious leather kink going on behind the stained glass windows of the B & B, but the whole town pretty much falls into three categories."

Kennedy's brow raised in question.

"Category one is for those who are against the leather or possibly even disgusted and repulsed by it. But, they've learned of some friends and family who attend, or they don't want to rock the delicate social balance of a small town—or their position in that social balance—so they keep quiet and only give me dirty looks when I see them around town." Category one people were always fun to run into. Awkward *polite* chitchat while the person burned through my soul with eyes of fiery condemnation.

"Yep, I've gotten plenty of those looks around town." Kennedy nodded. "But, it's awfully hard for others to pass judgement when they're being called to the station to pick up their kid for shoplifting, their husband for drunk driving, or their daughter for public indecency."

"I bet." I paused for a second, but Kennedy seemed to be waiting on me to continue. "Then there's category two. This is for the people who pretend they have no clue what goes on behind the doors on Sunday. Some of these people truly *are* clueless, but the majority are choosing to turn a blind eye. What they don't know can't hurt them. Some are truly deluding themselves while others are just too old or too naïve to understand."

"What about the third?" Kennedy shifted and leaned forward in the chair.

"Ahh, the third category is my favorite. Two types fit in this category. Type A is the kinky fucker who can't wait to get all leathered up, harnessed up, strapped up, and tied up. Also in Type A is the leather daddy who does the strapping and tying and flogging and fucking." Seeing men from every walk of life let loose and be themselves was a truly beautiful thing. "Type B though is sometimes the most fun to watch. They start out thinking they are just curious or coming to support a friend, and to maybe see what all the fuss is about. But time after time, I see the old adage of 'curiosity killed the cat'. Each Sunday they get a little braver, a little closer to the presentation, and a little more interested in the products or the discussions. Sometimes it stops there. Sometimes they end up finding out they are some of the kinkiest fuckers around and we've made a leather man for life." Realizing I'd gotten pretty wrapped up in shoptalk—as usual whenever discussing leather and kink—I smiled slightly through my heated cheeks and tried like hell to remember how much I hated Kennedy as he watched me wide-eyed.

"You change when you talk about leather Sundays. Your face totally lights up." Kennedy shook his head as if amazed at having pegged me.

"I feel good knowing I'm giving men an outlet, a place to be themselves, and a haven where they can connect with common spirits and desires." I didn't care that I sounded a bit sappy, leather Sundays were my baby and I was proud of what they meant to myself and so many others.

"Well, it definitely shows." Kennedy smiled. "Wait a second, did that just happen?"

"What?" I glanced around.

"Did we have an actual conversation without feeling weird or cussing each other out?" Kennedy placed a hand on his chest and gave a look of astonishment.

"Don't go ruining a good thing," I warned, but couldn't help the hint of a smile that pulled at my lips.

After a quiet moment, I stood and stretched. "Where the hell is Jay? I thought he was just ordering food?"

"He better not be looking at porn on my phone." Kennedy headed toward the stairs.

I laughed. "Jay may turn out to be a kinky little fuck, but I'm pretty sure he's keeping Levi so busy in bed neither of them would have the time or energy to look at porn right now."

"Are you fucking kidding me?" Kennedy groaned from the top of the stairs.

A loud thump sounded against the door.

"No?" I frowned as Kennedy stomped down the stairs. "They might like to look at porn together. I'm just saying I bet they are pretty satisfied."

"Not about the porn, jackass." He shoved a piece of paper in my face.

My Dearest Cody and Kennedy,

Don't ever forget how much I, *we*, love you. We've watched you dance around your attraction to each other with hatred and unsatisfying eye-fucking for much too long. This weekend is for your own good.

The pantry and fridge in the basement are completely stocked, as is the liquor cabinet. In the bedside table, you'll find condoms, lube, and a plethora of toys should you chose to include kinkery in your fuckery. The bathroom medicine cabinet has a bulk size pack of enemas for that not so fresh feeling. You know, they say 'cleanliness is next to godliness' so feel free to soap yo'selves up and get all squeaky clean before you do the dirty deed. Kennedy, since you likely don't have your cuffs on you, I took the liberty of providing cuffs, a rope, a flogger, and a ball gag in case the two of you decide to go full-on during your introductory period. There are several jock straps and undies for you to wear, model, and rip off with your teeth. While clothing is hopefully not needed, I have provided some loungewear for your convenience.

Yes, I do realize you'll likely kill me when this weekend is over. But, at least I'll know I died for a good cause. You two need to either admit your attraction and see if it's got true potential or fuck each other's brains out until you no longer burn with desire and anger every time you're together.

Please forgive me....hell, who am I kidding. When you two finally stop arguing long enough to realize something exists between you then you'll be bowing at my feet for bringing you together. Maybe even kissing my feet. Either of you have a foot fetish? I'd allow some ass slapping, as well.

So, the deal is you're in the basement until Sunday. Cody, your dad is covering the B & B for you. Micah, Cole, Levi, and myself will run the Sunday leather scene. If, by Sunday, you've not fucked yourselves into comas or agreed to at least be civil to each other, you may be required to stay extra days. I have no burning desire to let you out because I know my young, innocent life will be snuffed out much too soon.

Oh, I also ordered some pay-per-view gay porn and put it in the To-Watch list on the TV. You're welcome. Sometimes a little 'priming of the pump,' so to speak, works wonders in getting the juices flowing.

And don't try to pull one over on me. I know how a man walks when he's been thoroughly fucked. And I'm not above using a black light to check the basement for bodily fluids.

You two need to FUCK ALREADY and get it over with. It's like taking off a band-aid. Maybe a little scary, but ripping it off quickly hurts less than hem-hawing around and letting the wound fester under a nasty, dirty bandage.

With Much Love,

Jay

My jaw ached from clenching my teeth so hard, and I worked to control my breathing. Was this a fucking joke? The plan to kill and dismember Jay's body was back on. Totally back on.

"Damn little fucker took my phone." Kennedy grumbled. "Call Levi or Micah, tell them to get us out of here."

Cursing not-so-silently, I shook my head. "No can do. Left my phone in the truck with my bag."

"Fuck."

"Yep." I sighed and stomped up the stairs. Jay had played his little trick, but the joke was over. I pounded on the door. "Jay, you motherfucking sonofabitch open this piece of shit door *now*!"

"Cody, I find your name calling offensive. My mother definitely had issues and likely *could* be called a bitch. But I have never and will never fuck mothers of any type." Jay was silent for a moment. "Unless it's a drag queen dressed as mother, maybe I'd fuck her."

I slammed my hand against the door. "I swear to God, Jay, I will break this fucking door down if you don't let us out right this second."

"Sorry, no can do. This is seriously for your own good. I promise it will all be better in the end." Jay murmured something on the other side of the door.

"Are the guys out there?" No way my best friends would keep me locked in the fucking basement all weekend.

"Yeah, man, we're here," Levi answered.

I swore I heard a smile in his voice. "Open the damn door." My teeth would be ground to nothing after this. I kicked at the door. Damn solid oak.

"Hey, hey, careful with the door." Levi's stern words came through. "It's been through three generations of the Wells family. It's not replaceable, so no destroying my door."

"*Fuck!*" The word reverberated off the wood. "Where are Micah and Cole? Surely they've got some sense between the two of them."

"Gotta agree with Jay on this one, sorry."

Micah's words, too, held humor. Humor I was definitely *not* seeing in the situation.

"Can't say I'm in *total* agreement, but even if I was to vote no, I'd be outnumbered." Cole's words were the only ones that sounded the least bit apologetic.

"Pssst, Cody...," Jay staged a whisper behind the door. "The guys look like they want to punch me and hurt me. They are probably worried about their own lives after you kill me."

I heard chuckles quickly dissolve into a round of coughs.

"You damn little piece of shit. This isn't a joke," I growled.

"Watch it," Levi growled right back.

"We're going up to Micah and Cole's to work on The Blue Jay plans. We'll be back a couple times over the weekend to check on you. But, don't worry about keeping things quiet, because you've got the place to yourself."

Jay's words were *not* comforting. I didn't give a damn about privacy, I wanted to break free and wring the kid's neck. Then give Levi and Micah their fair share. But, the noises on the other side faded away until the only thing I could hear was complete and utter silence.

I was locked in a basement for an entire weekend with one of the only people on earth who literally pissed me off every time I was around him.

And my mind wouldn't stop playing images of him naked through my head.

Fuck.

CHAPTER 4

KENNEDY

Cody stomped down the stairs. "This isn't some fucking joke."

I grabbed a beer and plopped down on the couch to watch Cody's tirade.

Slam! The glasses in the small basement cabinet shook.

"They may have time for fun and games, but some of us have actual lives and careers."

Bang! The bathroom door slammed shut.

I feared the medicine cabinet mirror had shattered, but when Cody exited the bathroom, I saw no evidence of a cleanup needed. His fit carried on for about ten more minutes before he noticed me on the couch.

"Why the fuck aren't you mad? Did you know about this?" He advanced toward me, fists clenched.

"I swear to God, if I find out you had a part in this, I will fucking—"

"Whoa, dude, chill out." I held up my hands in defense, not really wanting to hear the rest of Cody's threat. "I swear I had nothing to do with this. Being locked in a basement on my weekend off with a guy who hates my guts is not my idea of fun and relaxing." Honestly, the situation was stacking up to be my worst nightmare sprinkled with my best fantasy. The images from my daydream the other day paraded through my mind. "I'm not thrilled with this situation, but if we're truly stuck here until Sunday, I figure there's not a whole lot we can do about it."

Cody studied me for a moment before unclenching his fists and sighing deeply. "Yeah, I guess purposely locking yourself in the basement with me would be about as high on your list of fun ways to spend a weekend as it would be on mine." He ran a hand through his hair and grasped the back of his neck. "What the hell are we going to do down here for," he glanced at the clock on the wall, "over forty-eight hours?"

"I guess we can just go with it. Take it like a vacation. Maybe get some plans worked out for The Blue Jay? They gave us really good beer and alcohol." I stood from the couch and walked to the kitchenette to open the freezer and fridge. "High-quality frozen pizza, lunchmeat, taco fixings, and a ton of other food." I turned to the tiny pantry. "Plenty in here to make some great breakfasts, gourmet coffee, and snacks out the wazoo." I spied a note taped to a bag of caramel and cheese popcorn.

I'm not a total monster. It's not as if you guys are prisoners. Okay, I mean, you sort of ARE prisoners, but that doesn't mean you have to eat bread and water. I want you guys to keep your energy up. Plus, food can make us happy. Maybe a big gooey cinnamon roll from the bakery in town along with some of the world's best coffee will keep you from killing me. ENJOY!

I couldn't help but laugh as I rolled my eyes and shook my head.

Cody grabbed the paper from me. After reading it, he growled, crumpled it, and threw it to the floor. "That damn smartass kid." But he opened the box on the counter to reveal four gigantic cinnamon rolls smothered in sweet, buttery, creamy icing. "Fuck if that doesn't look almost better than sex."

I peered over his shoulder. "Mmmm, breakfast tomorrow for sure."

"You hungry?" Cody turned toward me before I could step back and we found ourselves face-to-face.

The simple question, which I knew he meant absolutely *nothing* by, made my blood race as I breathed in his scent. Backing up slightly before I spoke, I cleared my throat. "I could eat."

I watched Cody's nostrils flare and his jaw clench. "I'll cook if you clean."

"What if I want to cook? You just automatically think I'm a girly man who will take the woman's spot in the kitchen?" My questions came out much cattier than I'd meant. Of course a big, built, masculine top like Cody would expect me to do his bidding.

"What?" Cody reared back and frowned. "Hell, no. I just meant we'd split the dinner duties. Would you rather cook?"

My cheeks pinked and I gave a sheepish smile. "No, you own a restaurant, you're likely much more talented in the kitchen than I am. I'll clean. Dishwasher is more my speed anyway."

Cody cocked his head to the side. "How about we both cook and both clean. Make it more fair that way."

"Someone once told me, 'The fair only comes in August and even then you have to pay.'" I shrugged. "Life isn't fair."

"Whatever." Cody scoffed. "French toast, pancakes, pizza, or tacos?"

My melancholy was pushed away as my stomach rumbled loudly. "French toast sounds really good. Did they leave any bacon?"

Cody checked the fridge. "Yep. The really good kind too." He pulled out the thick-sliced bacon before reaching for the eggs and milk. "Hey, they put strawberries in here."

"God, I love strawberries. Favorite fruit hands down." I grabbed the berries and washed them in the tiny sink.

"See if they remembered syrup." Cody pulled a skillet from the cabinet.

"I see chocolate syrup, but no…" I moved a bottle, "oh, here's the maple syrup."

"Mmmmm, chocolate syrup. We could make chocolate milkshakes." Cody opened the freezer and pointed at the tub of ice cream.

Gesturing to the bananas on the counter, I smiled. "Or banana splits."

"We'll be in food comas by the end of the weekend." Cody laughed and cracked an egg into a bowl.

"Not the type of blissed-out Jay had in mind, but sounds good to me." I handed Cody a whisk from the drawer.

"How stupid to think you and I were going to fuck each other's brains out just because we have to spend a couple days together?" Cody glanced over his shoulder.

"Yeah, we're grown men, pretty sure we have more control than that." I turned to get the loaf of thick-sliced artisan bread Jay had provided.

"Yeah, definitely," Cody mumbled. "Hey, which would you rather do? The toast or the bacon?"

"Oh, um, I'm sure I'd mess either or both up, you don't want me touching the food." I held my hands up in front of me to ward off his suggestion.

"The fuck you say. You've kept yourself fed and alive so far." Cody's gaze traveled from my head to my toes before meeting my eyes. "You look healthy, so I'd say you've done a decent job."

"I pretty much screw up everything, but I'll do whichever you think I can ruin the least."

Cody frowned. "You're one of the best officers in town, pretty sure you don't screw up *everything*. Here," he handed me the spatula, "you do the French toast, and I'll do the bacon. That way you're not getting popped with bacon grease."

"Hope you know what you're getting yourself into." I took over the French toast. "At least we'll have good bacon and strawberries if I burn this."

"And ice cream for dessert." Cody waggled his brows.

My heart caught. The more relaxed and flirty side of Cody was something I'd never really seen. It suited him. Too damn well. I ground my teeth and focused on flipping slices of golden brown bread. Cody and I would never work out. For all of my shortcomings, I was as stubborn and set in my ways as he was. Maybe we were just too much alike and that's why we had this friction between us. Either way, it was nice having a comfortable conversation, but that didn't mean he was done hating me.

"What?" Cody glanced my way.

"Huh?"

"You seem deep in thought."

"Oh, uh, just thinking it's nice not arguing with you." My cheeks warmed.

Cody nodded. "Yeah, I guess it is."

We cooked in silence for a moment.

"Fuck!" Cody jerked back from the frying pan and grabbed his eye.

"Shit, what happened?" I dropped the spatula and moved closer.

"Damn bacon grease popped in my eye."

"Here, let me see. Move to the bathroom where the light is better." I moved the frying pan to the back burner and turned down the toast.

In the bathroom, I turned my back to the sink and had Cody face me. "Move your hand so I can see."

"Don't touch it," Cody warned.

"Just let me see it first." I swallowed a laugh. Big, bad Cody was freaking out like a little kid with a splinter.

He removed his hand, but kept his eye firmly clenched shut.

"Can you open it?" I brushed a thumb over a red spot on his cheek. "You're red here. It may have gotten your cheek rather than your eye."

"Really?" Cody opened his eye.

"Good, opening it is good. It's not even red. Your eyelid isn't either." I shifted slightly so Cody could see in the mirror. "See? Just your cheek, and it's not even that bad."

"Stings like a bitch." Cody reached up to trace the red spot on his face.

"If there's honey, we can rub some on."

"Not butter?" Cody returned his gaze to mine.

Suddenly I was very aware of how close we were standing.

"Um, no butter. It traps the heat in. Honey is good because it's antibacterial." I shrugged. "At least that's what I've heard. Probably not true."

"Hey, don't do that." Cody brought his head down to make our eyes level.

"Do what?" I tried to turn away.

Cody stopped me. "That thing where you put yourself down and doubt yourself."

"Eh, it's about the only thing I'm good at." I forced a chuckle and attempted to slide away but Cody's arm blocked me.

"I don't think so. No man has ever argued with me as well as you do. You've been voted officer of the month more times than I can count. The town looks at you pretty much like their own superhero." Cody clenched his jaw.

"It's not like there are that many officers to get votes. And, most people look up to police officers. Those things are pretty much default." I pushed myself from the sink counter and choked on my gasp when my groin rocked into Cody's.

"That doesn't explain away your ability to argue with me." Cody stepped back from the contact.

"Oh, yeah, being the one person you love to hate is a real talent. I guess your arguments usually just piss me off so much I can't help but have something to say back." I turned to wash my hands.

"Shit, the food is going to burn," Cody dashed from the bathroom.

I caught up with him after drying my hands. "Nah, I turned it all down."

"See, you know what you're doing. I didn't even think about turning down the food." Cody patted his cheek. "Would have served Jay right though if we caught the basement on fire." He chuckled.

"Whatever. Let's just finish cooking this shit." I rinsed off the spatula. "You going to survive? Or do you need to go lay down?" I teased.

"Shut it, Marks. I'll be fine." Cody growled, but his usual hateful heat wasn't present.

We quickly realized two fairly large men in a tiny kitchen did not make for a graceful production.

"Ouch."

"Sorry," I shifted after stomping on Cody's foot.

"Damn it, sorry," Cody snapped.

"It's okay." I rubbed my back where he elbowed me when he moved to get the plates.

After we ran into each other three more times, Cody grabbed me by the shoulders. "You go set the table. I'll bring in the food."

I nodded. Glad to leave the miniature space, but immediately noticing the cool emptiness when Cody's hands left my shoulders.

By the time the table was set and the food brought in, I was starving.

We both dug into the meal.

"Damn, this is good." I spoke between mouthfuls. "You should totally start a breakfast menu at the B & B."

"Micah and Cole said the same thing." Cody chewed and seemed to think it over. "I guess a brunch menu could be pretty cool and bring in some more customers who usually go to the coffee shop or bakery."

"Definitely would bring in more people. Maybe start with just Saturday and Sunday brunch. Then see if you want to expand to the weekdays." I took a long swig of milk.

"It's worth a thought." Cody nodded.

As we carried our dishes over to the sink, Cody glanced around. "God this space is tiny when you're trying to fit more than one person." He found a dishtowel. "You want to wash or dry?"

"I'll wash." I ran the sink full of hot water and added soap.

Within fifteen minutes we had the kitchenette completely cleaned up.

"You want ice cream now or later?" Cody raised his brows.

"Ugh, too stuffed. Later." I rubbed my belly and sauntered to the couch. "Maybe there's a decent movie?"

Cody shouldered me out of the way and grabbed the remote. "What kind of movies do you like?"

"Mysteries, police dramas, suspense, that type of thing."

Cody rolled his eyes. "You would," he huffed.

"What's wrong with movies like that?" My defenses were on guard.

"Action movies is where it's at. War, gore, real-life type stuff." Cody began flipping through the guide. "I don't want to have to think and solve a damn suspense or mystery while I'm watching a movie. Movies are supposed to be entertaining, not thought-provoking."

I snorted. "Wow, that's possibly the dumbest thing I've ever heard you say. Yeah, watch out for those damn thought-provoking movies that make you use your brain." I cocked my head. "Are you serious right now or just trying to get into an argument?"

Cody lifted a shoulder. "I like action movies. End of story."

"No argument there, action movies are good. You asked what I liked, I told you. No reason to get shitty because our taste in movies is different."

"Not shitty, just proves we got nothing in common." Cody landed on a movie that definitely looked like his type. "How about this? Looks like action but maybe some suspense too."

"As long as you won't hurt yourself trying to think while we watch it." I couldn't hold back the sarcasm. The man was infuriating.

"Fuck off." Cody selected *Play* on the screen.

And just like that, we were back to our old selves.

CHAPTER 5

CODY

Shit. There's nothing I hate more than feeling like I've lost control of a situation. So being locked in a basement with a guy I could barely stand was bad enough, but throw in the fact that we actually got along for a while—albeit clumsily—together in the kitchen, and the hot-as-fuck Nurse Kennedy and Patient Cody scenario in the bathroom and my world was spinning out of control and straight into chaos.

I had to get us back to status quo. Picking an argument was easy.

Fighting with Kennedy was my norm. I'd never asked why, because I'd never have a solid answer. We'd always been oil and water—the gasoline to each other's fire.

I flipped Kennedy the bird as we settled in to watch some stupid-ass movie. I hated the fact that Kennedy liked the same types of movies as me, but I would never admit to it. So, I sat back, pretended to be into the action flick, and did my best to ignore the sexy-as-sin Officer Marks seated only feet away.

About thirty minutes into the movie, Kennedy stood up. "I'm ready for ice cream. You want something?"

I refused to let on that the movie was boring me to death, so I ignored him for a few seconds until the scene ended and then clicked *Pause*. "Yeah, ice cream sounds good." I stood up, grateful to stretch.

Kennedy turned toward the kitchen and went straight for the pantry. Producing the bottle of chocolate syrup, he shook it and smiled. "How about chocolate shakes?"

Following him to the kitchen, I went to the alcohol. I gave the liquor selection a quick perusal. "How about Mudslides?" I mimicked his actions with a bottle of vodka in one hand and Kahlua in the other.

"Good call." Kennedy reached for the blender. "You know, living down here wouldn't be half bad if they kept it stocked. And, you know, didn't make you a prisoner."

"Yeah, pretty sure this little space has never been stocked so well. Jay pulled out all the stops for sure." I pulled the ice cream from the freezer.

Several shots of vodka and Kahlua were consumed before the Mudslides were actually made. By the time we turned our backs on a sink full of chocolate covered stickiness and headed back to watch the movie, I was just beyond buzzed. Which meant I had partaken in more than my share of shots because it took a lot to get me buzzed. When Kennedy stumbled as he rounded the corner of the couch, I figured he'd overdone the shots, as well. But, the smooth, sweet, chocolate shakes went down super easy and before too long the movie was forgotten and Kennedy and I were trading snarky comments and barbs.

"You'd never be able to work at the B & B, you'd waste way too much alcohol if you made all drinks with as heavy of a hand as you made these.

Damn, how much did you put in?" My head was definitely fuzzy, but I nursed that icy concoction like my life depended on it.

"Fuck you. You're just mad I make a better drink than you." Kennedy made a *cheers* gesture in the air before slurping down more of his Mudslide.

"Whatever, I'd school you every which way when it comes to mixing drinks and running a restaurant." My head lolled back against the couch.

"Maybe the first few times, but I'm a quick learner." Kennedy's head flopped against the couch, as well and he turned his head turned toward me with a smile. "I'd take over the B & B within months if you ever trained me and turned me loose."

"The fuck you say. You ever run a restaurant? Mix drinks behind a busy bar? Take orders and cook for an entire crowd of hungry people?" I didn't like Kennedy insinuating he could do my job better than me.

"Eh, can't be that hard. *You* do it." A challenging glint lit Kennedy's eyes.

"Tell me something, Marks, do you plan the words that come out of your mouth just to piss me off, or is it a coincidence that every time you speak I end up wanting to bust your ass?" I slammed the empty beer mug down, the sweet ice cream treat now gone and all of the alcohol was playing games in my head.

"Guess I'm just lucky." Kennedy shrugged.

I watched him for a moment. "God, I wish I knew why I hate you so much."

"Guess I'm just lucky." Kennedy shrugged again. "Pretty much the story of my life."

"What's that mean?" I probably could have curled up and slept on that couch until morning. The movie credits were rolling, the alcohol had me all warm and fuzzy, and as fucked up as Kennedy and I were together, I was comfortable and calm.

"Just that people have hated me since I was born." Kennedy sighed and placed his empty mug on the coffee table next to mine.

"Why?"

"My mom and dad were beyond fucked up. My dad raped my mom in a drunken rage, and he hated me from the moment I was conceived. He hated my mother but kept her around to abuse and fuck when he wasn't out with other women. From the day I was born, she did her best to protect me, but she was often too weak or injured to save me, especially the older I got. He pretty much beat me or verbally attacked me every day of my life until they both died."

"Shit, man, that sucks. I'm sorry." My heart hurt for the young kid Kennedy had been and what he'd experienced. There was likely more to the story about his parents, but Kennedy didn't appear to be in the storytelling mood.

"Yeah, well, I ended up with much better parents. So it wasn't all bad. But, I'm used to people hating me. I think that's why I don't get too upset when people get angry or call me names on the job. I'm used to it. Numb, maybe?" Kennedy rubbed his eyes. "Look at me, I'm not someone anyone would fear or cower to."

"Wait, are you saying the only reason people like *me* is because of my size and tough demeanor? People fear me or cower to me and that's why I have friends?" My heart still hurt for him, but he was pissing me off again.

"I guess if the shoe fits." Kennedy slurred his words.

"That's a bunch of bullshit. I have friends because I'm a good guy, and I take care of the people I love." The conversation was seriously going nowhere.

"So, if I was a good guy I'd have friends even though I look like a sub bottom?" Kennedy wasn't making any sense.

"You being a bottom or a sub has nothing to do with anything. Just like me looking like a top or a dom has nothing to do with anything." I ran a hand over my face. "God, I think we are way too drunk to be having this conversation."

"Yeah, probably." Kennedy agreed and then fell silent. The last thing I heard before I fell into a drunken sleep was a snore as Kennedy joined me.

I had no clue how long I'd been asleep, but I woke in a curled, cramped position with a furnace wrapped around me. Kennedy's arms held me like one would hold a lover, full body contact. My mouth was dry, my head throbbed, but all of my attention was directed to Kennedy's warmth. How in the hell had I ended up in his arms? How and when had we stretched out on the couch, our bodies being forced together by the sheer narrowness of the furniture?

Kennedy's lips were mere inches from my neck, so close I felt the heat of his breath on my skin. I could turn in his arms and crush him to the cushions, ravish his mouth, explore his body, end the ridiculousness of Jay's plan.

Or.

Or, I could shift under him and let his body pin me, trap me. A shiver of confused anticipation traveled through my veins. Kennedy wasn't the type to take charge and dominate a sexual situation, was he? And, when had I ever wanted that? Never, that's when. Maybe I was still drunk.

Kennedy's hand moved until it found mine and grasped it firmly.

Holy hell.

No way. Bad enough I had no clue how we ended up cuddling, but no way was I letting him wake up to me curled in his arms like an infant.

I bolted upright and stood from the couch, all but sprinting to the bathroom in hopes Kennedy wouldn't wake completely until I was out of the small living room.

CHAPTER 6

KENNEDY

Waking up to find Cody wrapped in my arms, our bodies pressed together and cuddled like lovers, was one of the best and worst moments of my life.

It felt good. It felt right. So damn right to hold him, protectively, in my embrace.

But it would never happen for real. Could. Never. Happen. Cody wasn't the type to need protecting, to need controlled, to need challenged and dominated and punished.

Fuck, how I wanted that.

As I lay awake but pretending to sleep while feeling Cody's body come to life, I imagined what his skin would taste like if I were to lean in to kiss his neck, to whisper against his ear, to grasp his chin and force his mouth to mine for a searing kiss.

Cody could easily overpower me—and I'd enjoy it. Being pinned under his strong, beautiful body would be no hardship. Having him top me would be some of the best sex I'd ever had, I was sure of it.

But, my heart wasn't in it. Sex, even not-great sex, was almost always enjoyable. But, my heart craved something else. I longed for Cody's strength, control, and dominance to give in to me and to be mine. I wanted to own him—his pleasure and his pain. I wanted it all to myself.

And damn if that didn't confuse the fuck out of me. I'd always considered myself "vers," but more on the bottom side. And when it came to leather play, I never played any role but the submissive bottom. So why was my mind such a clusterfuck of thoughts and images of me dominating a dominant?

I drifted in and out of sleep to the sound of the shower coming on. When I woke again, keeping up my ruse of still being asleep, I heard the sound of the bathroom door opening. My guess was Cody was now in the kitchen getting coffee going. And maybe some breakfast to nurse my hangover. Damn alcohol and sweets delivered a shitty headache.

I needed to piss and brush my teeth before I could even think about facing Cody. No clue how he was going to play off this morning. He couldn't have liked waking up in my arms.

Rolling from the couch, morning wood pressed tightly behind my zipper, I shuffled to the bathroom while rubbing sleep from my eyes.

And walked right in on Cody in nothing but a jockstrap.

I had clearly been mistaken about him leaving the bathroom.

"Fuck, sorry." I meant to back from the room and turn around. I meant to. But, my sleepy eyes and hungover mind couldn't follow through. Instead, I stood and stared at Cody. His broad chest sprinkled with dark hair, his cock—sporting its own morning wood, if I wasn't mistaken—cupped tightly in the pocket of the jock.

Damn, I wanted him to turn around so I could see that round, firm bubble butt encased in elastic.

"Take a picture, it'll last longer." Cody sneered.

The comment broke my reverie and forced a laugh from me. "What is this, PeeWee, the eighties?"

"Fuck you, man." Cody grabbed a tank top from the sink and covered his beautiful body before shouldering past me. "Move it. I need coffee."

"Nice panties." I couldn't help it. Fucking with Cody Parker was one thing I was not only good at but I enjoyed immensely. My eyes were glued to his ass as it jiggled slightly in a sexy-as-fuck little tease as he walked away.

"Shut it. Jay only left us jocks and tanks. Damn little fucker." Cody started slamming things around in the kitchen in his quest for coffee.

While I very much appreciated Jay's choice of clothing on Cody, I wasn't pleased that I'd have to be in a tank and jock around Cody for the rest of the weekend. At least my jeans were still fairly clean. I turned on the shower, undressed quickly, and climbed in. The warm water soothed my head and the fresh scent of soap along with the aroma of coffee wafting through the air promised I'd live to see another day. As long as Jay had left me a toothbrush, I'd make the most of my prison time.

I finished my shower and found the tank and jock Jay had left and pulled them both on before donning my jeans. I wandered into the kitchen to find Cody, thankfully back in his jeans as well, pouring himself a cup of coffee.

"You better catch up. This is cup two for me." Cody lifted his mug. "Wasn't sure how you take yours, but there's cream and sugar if you want it."

"Nah, black is fine." I raised and lowered a shoulder.

"That how you like it?" Cody cocked a brow.

"No, love it with cream and butter."

"The fuck you say. Butter? That's disgusting." Cody curled up his nose.

"I thought so too, until a guy at work got me to try it." I shrugged. "It's called Bulletproof coffee. I don't drink it often, but it's so damn good. Rich and creamy and supposedly pretty healthy for you."

"Well, now you've gone and piqued my interest." Cody opened the fridge and began rummaging around. "Like, margarine or real butter?"

"Real butter, preferably unsalted." I smiled. "It's best if we can mix it up in a blender type thing." I scoured the cabinets until I found a food processor. "This will work."

Cody threw a stick of butter on the counter before reaching back into the refrigerator for the cream. "Is heavy whipping cream okay?"

"Yeah, that's the best. Other cream doesn't work as well, doesn't make it as creamy." I poured the cream into the processor and spooned in some chunks of butter. "If we wanted to make it truly tasty, we'd slip in come coconut oil. But, I doubt Jay stocked that and it's almost just as good without it."

"I can't believe I'm getting ready to drink coffee with *butter* in it." Cody shivered.

I laughed. "Oh ye of little faith. You never know unless you try it. It may turn out to be your favorite coffee drink ever." I poured the hot coffee over the butter and cream and placed the lid on top. Flipping on the switch, I let the mixture spin and froth for about fifteen seconds. "Okay, you'll have to sweeten it to your taste, but here ya go." I waited for Cody to pour out the last couple swigs of his coffee and hold his mug out for me to fill.

He mixed in his sweetener. "Is this stuff counteracting the healthy part?"

"Nah, that's stevia extract, so it's a natural sweetener." I doctored my own coffee and held it to my nose before breathing deeply. "Oh my God. I haven't made this in months. It smells so good. There's no way you won't like it. It's also to die for in hot tea."

Cody sniffed his cup's content before taking his first sip. With his second sip, his gaze met mine over the rim of the cup and his eyes lit up. "That's the best damn coffee I've ever had."

"Right?" I smiled. "Sounds gross, but so good." I savored my own cup of creamy deliciousness.

"I should put this on the menu." Cody closed his eyes as he drank more of the concoction. "People would love it."

"Definitely. Especially if you pair it with some breakfast options." I winked.

"Yeah, yeah, I hear ya." Cody sauntered into the living room. "What the fuck are we going to do all day?"

"We could actually plan some suggestions and ideas for The Blue Jay." I lifted a shoulder. "Not like we've got a whole lot of other choices."

"As much as I hate to do anything for Owens right now, you're right. The Blue Jay is going to be good for the young people in and around BJ. Let's get busy." Cody nodded his head toward the tiny table.

"No way we're both fitting there with paper, pens, coffee, and ourselves." I glanced around. Grabbing a notepad from the coffee table, I tore off a few pieces for myself and found a book to use as a base. "Here, you can have the pad. Let's see if any pens are around here."

We got situated on the couch with our tools and coffee.

"Okay, so what are your thoughts?" Cody wrote The Blue Jay across the top of his notepaper.

"First, I think we have to be sure it appeals to the locals as well as others. With this being a railroad town, a lot of families come here to work and are just happy to have a job. They don't want their kids getting involved with anything that looks like trouble. The locals will want it to have a helpful community feel to it. But, the Blue Jay needs to be universally welcoming to the newer folks, tweens, and teens from nearby towns. The BJ should be a place where a parent is happy to drop off their kid." I rattled off my thoughts.

"Gee, you've been thinking on this some, haven't you?" Cody's eyes were wide and a small smile graced his face.

"Yeah, guess so. My childhood sucked. A place like The Blue Jay would have been helpful." I shrugged.

"Okay, I like where you're going. One thing I was thinking about, if we want to pull in kids from neighboring towns, we might have to think of transportation. If these kids are from troubled homes and need support, they likely won't have a parent willing to drive them to BJ and pick them up. I was thinking we could find a bus and have Micah spruce it up. Get our bus permits and someone could pick up kids who need a ride." Cody sketched little doodles on his paper as he spoke.

"Yeah, that's good. Lots of insurance issues and liability to deal with. Maybe instead of a bus, just a van?" I was thinking of legalities and logistics. "Or, there's a county transport service. Maybe we provide the kids from outside of BJ with transport cards so they can catch a ride to and from?" I made notes.

"That's a good one." Cody added it to his list. "What about food?"

"Hmm, it *would* be awesome if we knew someone with ties to a restaurant who could help out in that area." I tapped my chin, pretending to ponder.

"Shut it. I'll provide food as often as possible. No problem with that. But, the kids will need snacks. Maybe some canned and boxed goods from time to time if food isn't plentiful at home?" Cody chewed the end of his pen. "We could get some reusable bags and fill them up with non-perishables. If a kid needs a bag, they take it. Bring it back when they need more. I bet the businesses around town would donate bags, supplies, and money."

"Laundry soap and toiletries, as well." I recalled trying to do my laundry at age eight. I'd spilled something on myself at lunch and knew I'd be made fun of if I came back to school with the stained shirt, so I attempted to wash it. But we had no laundry soap so I'd tried to use dish soap. Got one of the worst beatings of my life when my father saw the mess of suds overflowing the washer.

"Yeah, like deodorant, shampoo, soap. Razors, feminine stuff, toothpaste and toothbrushes. I bet Sadie would *love* to help put together little care packages." Cody mused and smiled. The guy couldn't ever talk about his little sister without getting that mushy big brother look on his face.

"Okay, what about homework help?" I made another note on my growing list of ideas.

"Definitely." Cody made his own notes. "I'm sure Cole will be willing to tutor."

"But Cole can't do it all himself."

"No, but he'd be a good one to find others to volunteer some tutoring hours. He's got connections at the high school and the elementary and middle schools." Cody pursed his lips. "I bet my parents would be willing to help out. Micah's mom would too. Sadie would give some hours. I bet some honors class students at the high school would volunteer. It would look good on their college applications."

"Okay, and recreation can be as simple as some video games and computer games. Put up some basketball goals outside. Maybe have some weight machines or free weights." I scribbled more notes. "What about social services or counseling or something like that?"

Cody pinned me with his gaze. "I'm guessing that type of thing would be really helpful, but would the kids be willing to take part in that?"

Cody seemed to be asking about my past without actually asking.

"I would have balked if it was introduced straight up as therapy or counseling. But, if someone had been there just to talk or offer advice or just be a friend, I would have been more open to it." I thought back to how fucked up my head was and how I fought therapy for such a long time after my parents' death. "We could talk to the social workers and counselors at the schools and the medical center. See if any of them would like to give an hour or so here and there to get to know the kids. Have them available if there's a need. Sort of like having them as consultants if serious concerns and issues exist or occur."

"I think these are some great ideas." Cody tapped the pen against his notepad. "One of the biggest things is funding. Jay has the start up money, but we need to plan ahead for fundraisers, donations from the community, and even looking into donations from outside of BJ, ya know?"

"Agreed." I nodded. "I was thinking the usual car washes, softball tourneys, bake sales, maybe a community yard sale? Have The Blue Jay kids help if possible with fundraisers, as well. Not expecting them to sell things, but have them wash cars, work the yard sale, that type of thing."

"I know Jay's planning on having dance classes, painting and other art instruction, and a library of sorts. But, I think he can take care of the details with all of that since that's his area of expertise." Cody flipped through his notes. "What about having officers give some volunteer hours? Or stop by to interact when their shifts allow?"

"Definitely. I'd be more than willing and so would most of the guys." Building relationships, especially the younger generation, was very important to our department.

"I'm even thinking about, further down the road, maybe setting up some job shadowing or internship type positions for the kids at The Blue Jay who are looking at future careers. Need to have kids ready for the three E's, education, enlistment, employment. Not everyone is cut out for college, but they need to know their options." Cody rolled his neck and yawned.

"Speaking of that, what about getting some of the military branches to send information or recruitment officers to speak to the kids who are interested?" Enlisting in the military wasn't something I'd thought about before, but that option was a fantastic opportunity for many young people.

Cody scribbled more notes. "Also, besides the six BJ Boys, we could have members of the LGBTQ+ community visit and give of their time. Some of these kids are searching for who they really are, and we need to provide them with positive role models."

"I like it." I chewed my bottom lip and felt a swell of pride to be included in the BJ Boys label. "I know Jay made up this 'idea session' as a ruse to get us in the basement, but I think he'll be impressed with our plans."

"Yeah, too bad he'll be dead and buried and unable to execute any of them." Cody groused.

"We can't kill him, but we should definitely give him as much shit as possible for a very long time." I chuckled. "I mean, I know you still hate me, but at least him locking us down here has proven that we can be in the same general vicinity as each other without throwing punches."

"True. I guess that's one good thing that came from Twinky Twinkerbell's meddling." Cody rolled his eyes.

"You know, that nickname could be offensive in many instances, but it fits Jay perfectly, I can't be mad." I smiled at the thought of our young, flashy friend.

"He loves the nickname. Says he owns it and knows just how to work it." Cody shook his head but couldn't hide his smile. "That kid is something else."

"He has a huge and well-intentioned heart even though his actions and motives are sometimes slightly misplaced." I tossed my paper and pen to the ground. "I'm bored. What do we do now?"

Cody threw his own notepad to the side. "How 'bout some porn?"

CHAPTER 7

CODY

"Did you seriously just say we should watch porn?" Kennedy stared at me in shock. Or maybe disgust. Possibly shocked disgust.

I shrugged. "What? I'm sure Jay spent a nice little chunk of cash to get some really good stuff. We might as well take advantage of premium pornography."

"Just when I start to think you may not actually be the piggish asshole my mind has made you out to be, you go and suggest we watch porn. We're grown men, locked in a basement, trying to make plans for a *youth center* and you want to watch X-rated movies?" Kennedy's brow scrunched.

"Nah," I started.

Kennedy let out a breath that I took to be relief.

"Jay probably got the triple X content." It took everything in me to say the words without busting out in laughter. Kennedy's face registered complete and utter disbelief, and he growled as he launched himself from the couch and stomped into the kitchen.

"You're fucking unbelievable," he called out as he slammed dishes around.

"What?" I hollered. Chuckling softly to myself, I stood and walked toward the kitchen to join him. "Just hear me out."

What in the ever loving hell was I doing?

"Yes, please, oh wise one. Share your sacred knowledge of how watching porn will improve our situation."

"You know what? Never mind. I didn't realize it before, but I get it now. I won't force you." I held up my hands in surrender.

"Didn't realize what?" Kennedy asked as I walked away. "No, come back here. You didn't realize what?"

People who don't like each other much, or at least have never figured out any way to get along due to their extreme dislike of the other should *never* be locked in a basement together. It causes stir-craziness, stupidity, and impulsiveness along with childish behavior. That's the only way I could explain what I was doing.

"I was thinking about how my suggestion of watching some mind-numbing, harmless, innocent porn shouldn't be such an issue for you. I guess I didn't realize how much it would threaten you and make you uncomfortable." I shook my head. "No big deal. I won't do anything to put you in an upsetting situation."

Kennedy placed both hands on his lean hips, his mouth opening and closing like a goldfish gasping for air. When he finally spoke, his voice was low. "Whoa, hold up. Are you insinuating I'm *scared* to watch porn?"

"Sometimes if the shoe fits you've just got to wear it even if you don't think it's your style." As the words tumbled out of my mouth, I flinched at how accurately they hit home personally.

"No way am I scared to watch porn with you." Kennedy stalked to the couch and grabbed the remote. "I think it's a bad idea, but I'm not scared." He took a step closer to me and jabbed my chest. "Not scared of you or your damn dares either."

Fuck. I wanted Kennedy to get rough with me, to hurt me, and then take it all away with caressing pleasure. "Let's go then." I wrestled the remote from his hand and plopped down on the couch just as a knock sounded at the basement door.

Kennedy and I looked at each other and bolted toward the steps. Taking the stairs two at a time, we almost knocked each other over.

"Jay? You goddamn little fucker, let us out of here right now!" I roared and pounded the door.

"Jay, seriously, this has gone on long enough." Kennedy spoke calmly like one would imagine an officer speaking to a scared child or a hostage taker. "We don't even hate each other anymore." Kennedy's gaze met mine, his eyes begging me to agree with him.

Crowded at the top of the stairs, our bodies mere inches apart, close enough I could feel his breath against my skin, I could only nod. "Yeah, man. Your plan worked. We learned our lesson and can get along now."

Absolute silence greeted us from the other side of the old wooden door, but a slip of paper poked between our feet.

Kennedy sighed and plodded back down the stairs while I picked up the note.

Is it done? Did you two fuck like bunnies and get it over with? Why do you think the expression is always about bunnies and rabbits fucking? Do members of the rabbit family have the record for fucking the most? Or the best? I've always wondered about that. What about other rodents? Bunnies are rodents, right? I mean, you never hear anyone refer to 'fucking like moles' or 'fucking like mice.' Always just rabbits or bunnies.

Anyway, I'm guessing you two haven't consummated your relationship. That's okay. I didn't think it would happen right away. It's a shame though because I bet you could be burning up the sheets and having a lot more fun than you're probably having arguing and bickering.

Levi says you're both too damn stubborn for your own good. Micah says you'll never give in and fuck it out because it would prove me right. Cole says I've gone about this the wrong way. But I have faith in you two. I know you're scared to admit it, but you two are crazy attracted to each other. I see it and I feel it. It radiates from you whenever you're near the other.

Embrace the fear, take doubt by the horns, summon all your courage, use those God-given balls...and fuck each other already. I don't HAVE to let you out on Sunday. You've got enough food down there for at least a few weeks. I'm just sayin'.

Love you both. Stop fighting it.

Jay

"You know what? I'm about ready to say fuck it and get it over with." I crumpled up the paper and threw it to the ground. The effect wasn't nearly as loud, pounding, and satisfying as I hoped it would be.

"Well, that's a beautiful and inviting request, but since two people need to agree to the aforementioned fucking, I think you're shit out of luck." Kennedy folded both arms across his chest.

"Whatever, it's not like I'd force you. But, you know sex between us would be good, even if it was bad." Why in the hell was I trying to persuade a man I despised just yesterday into having sex with me?

"Wow, you really know how to flatter and impress with your flowery words." Kennedy rolled his eyes and turned away. He kept his arms crossed as he flopped down onto the couch. "Let's just watch the damn porn. Maybe it will bore me to sleep. I just want this damn weekend over with."

I flung my arm toward the stairs. "Well, if the fucking dungeon master has his way we'll be locked down here until we fuck or our dicks fall off. I don't plan on the latter, so maybe the former is our best bet. Do it, enjoy it, get it over with, and then get on with our lives."

Kennedy glared.

"Whatever. But, don't say no just yet. Think about it while we watch." I flipped the channel to the pay-per-view only to find a large selection of gay porn videos ready and waiting for our perusal and viewing pleasure. "Jesus Christ, he must have spent over a hundred dollars on all these titles." I started scrolling. "Stop me if something catches your eye."

As I moved through the titles, I wasn't sure whether to laugh or get more pissed at Jay than I already was.

Friends to Fuckers
I Hate You, I Fuck You
My Enemy In Me
Fool Me Once, Fuck Me Twice
Love Is a Battlefield
Butt Stabber

Bareback Betrayal

Heinous Anus

Frenemies with Benefits

"Are you fucking kidding me?" Kennedy snorted.

"Creative little fucker, huh?" I smirked and cast a quick glance Kennedy's way.

"For fuck's sake, just pick one." Kennedy shook his head and settled in with a scowl.

I did a few random up and down clicks and landed on *My Enemy In Me*. "Screw it. This is probably as good or bad as any of the others."

"Let's just get it over with." Kennedy turned a frown my way. "Remind me again why I'm trying to prove I'm not scared to watch porn with you."

"Because you're a guy who doesn't back down from a challenge?"

Kennedy huffed. "Yeah, well, backing down is my forte. I don't usually care about proving myself.

I gave up on that long ago when I realized I'd never be what anyone wanted."

I nearly gave myself whiplash as I jerked my head to see if Kennedy was joking.

Nope.

"What the hell man? How do you go from arguing with me like your life depends on it to slamming yourself in mere seconds?" My brain couldn't quite grasp whether I was angry *at* him or hurt *for* him.

"Eh, long story that happened an even longer time ago. And I'd need a shit ton of alcohol to ever get into all of it." Kennedy shook his head and waved it off. "Sorry, shouldn't have even mentioned it."

"Whatever." I turned back to the television screen. "But, if we're attempting not to hate each other maybe we should revisit this conversation some day with copious amounts of alcohol."

"Just play the damn movie," Kennedy grumbled.

Forty-five minutes later the credits rolled. Kennedy and I finally glanced at each other.

"Damn, I really hope he didn't spend a lot on that one." Kennedy wrinkled his nose. "Or maybe I just don't know good porn when I see it."

"No, that sucked. Hard. And not in a good way." I flipped through some of the other titles.

"Dude, if we're going to watch another one, I'll need some alcohol. I can't do another bad movie, even with hot ass and dick, while I'm stone cold sober." Kennedy stood from the couch and headed toward the kitchen.

"Agreed. Alcohol will at least make us feel better even if the next one is as bad." I followed.

"The dudes were attractive, but the premise of the film was ridiculous and the acting was terrible." Kennedy rummaged through the liquor selection. "How about shots and then some of that pricey, high-end import beer Jay put in the fridge to soothe his captives?"

"What did he even put in there?"

Kennedy stuck his head in the refrigerator, his sexy ass bent at the perfect angle. "I'm not a beer expert, but it's definitely an import. Sapporo's Space Barley?"

"Damn." I whistled. "That shit is like a hundred dollars for a six-pack."

"You're kidding," Kennedy shot me a wide-eyed look.

"Nope. I'm in the business of beer, I know things." I winked.

"Then I say we drink it all. Every last drop of expensiveness." Kennedy rubbed his hands together and pulled the six-pack from the fridge.

"I'm game." I got eight shot glasses from the cabinet. "What are we shooting?"

"Any flavored vodka?"

"No." I moved more bottles around. "What about Fireball?"

"That will work."

I set up the glasses and filled all eight shots.

We clinked glasses.

The first shot went down rough and on fire.

"We should bring snacks to the movie," Kennedy suggested.

"Shots first." I raised glass number two. "To better porn and getting the hell out of this basement."

"Cheers!" Kennedy raised his glass.

Shot two went down smoother.

"Holy hell, that burns." Kennedy grimaced. "But it's a good burn."

"Pretty sure 'it's a good burn' is a quote in at least one of the videos we've got to watch." I laughed, my brain feeling warm and cozy.

Kennedy raised glass three. "To enemies and lovers."

I cocked my brow at his choice of words.

"In the movies," Kennedy sputtered, his words a little thick.

We took our shots.

"Damn, maybe we should have eaten something *before* the shots. I'm already buzzed." Kennedy reached for his final shot but stumbled.

"Whoa, let's hold off then." I grabbed his arm.

"Nope, last one will go down smoooooth," Kennedy drawled. "Go down smooth." He laughed. "I go down smooth."

I smiled and picked up my last shot. "To going down smooth." I raised my glass.

"Mmm, sounds good." Kennedy shot the amber liquid and slammed the glass down on the table before leaning into me. Chest to chest, he smiled. "Do you go down smooth?"

"I'm going to pretend you didn't just ask me that because there are *way* too many ways I could take it." I turned him by his shoulders toward the couch and television. "I think you're a little more than buzzed. No beer for now." I returned the six-pack to the refrigerator before joining a glassy-eyed Kennedy on the couch. "You still want to watch something?"

He lolled his head against the back of the couch and turned a silly grin my way. "Yeppers. Sober porn sucked. But I think drunk porn is going to be much better."

Fuck me all to hell. Was he flirting? We were both buzzed, but him more so than me. It would be irresponsible to take advantage of him if he wasn't absolutely one hundred percent coherent.

But damn those eyes and that goofy grin.

I scrolled through the titles in hopes of picking a good one.

"Mmmm, Bareback Betrayal." Kennedy moaned. "Who doesn't love a little bareback fun?"

Fuck me sideways. Drunk Kennedy was a handful.

And damn if it didn't turn me on.

"Bareback it is then." I cleared my throat and started the video.

Fortunately, or unfortunately depending on how one chose to look at the situation, *Bareback Betrayal* was actually a top quality video with above-average acting, a decent storyline, and hot-as-fuck actors who portrayed a real chemistry on-screen.

And fuck if I wasn't horny as hell sitting on a couch next to an even hotter guy. Who at that moment appeared to be as turned on as I was based on his continued flirting and fiery glances.

No. Kennedy and I had no business hooking up.

And if we hooked up, Jay would win.

I wouldn't let Jay's little trick work.

Jay may have locked us in the basement, but I was still in control and could keep my primal urges under wraps in my pants—pants that were getting tighter by the second.

And then Kennedy had to go and rub his fly as if he needed to relieve pressure of his own.

If I decided to hook up with Kennedy, and if Kennedy made the same decision, then the whole situation would still be in our control. *Us* calling the shots.

Yeah, we'd just be two consenting adults who decided to help each other scratch an itch.

Jay and the others could be damned.

Kennedy snorted at something on the screen, ground the heel of his hand against his jeans again, and hiccupped before turning my way. "I may be drunk, and this may be stupid, like really stupid. Beyond stupid."

I raised a brow and waited.

"But maybe you're right. We just do it and get it over with. That way we're out of here sooner and can get back to our normal lives. Maybe without the hatred and constant arguing, but just do it, get it out of our systems, move on." Kennedy's words slurred as he strung his thoughts together.

"So, you're admitting you've got it in your system to fuck me?" I teased.

"Shut up, you know you'd love a piece of this ass." Kennedy rolled to his side to face me and slapped his backside.

"Well, while I like the fact that you're agreeing that I'm right, I think you've had way too much to drink to make a hookup completely consensual at this point in time." I hated what I was saying, but the thought of us having sex was strange enough, doing it while Kennedy was past buzzed was just wrong.

"I'm not drunk," Kennedy protested.

"Mmmhmm," I hummed before smiling. "Your eyes are just bright enough to be considered glassy, your words are getting thick, and you're extremely flirty when you've been imbibing, Officer."

Kennedy bit his bottom lip and lowered his head before lifting eyes alight with heat my way. "You know what else is getting thick?"

"Jesus fuck, you can't say things like that." I shifted uncomfortably on the couch and reminded myself one of us had to be responsible. "Maybe let's sober up a little then we can revisit this idea."

Kennedy crossed both arms over his chest and pouted his bottom lip before a wicked gleam filled his face. In a flash, Kennedy had grasped the back of my neck and pulled me close. "Fine, but I want a kiss to hold me over."

Kennedy's warm, wet mouth was beyond my wildest imagination. Dear God, had I ever tasted a sweeter mouth? Been pulled under by a hotter kiss? Shivered at the moan of a sexier man? Never had a kiss held such explosive power and possibility.

Kennedy pulled back slightly, resting his forehead against mine. "Holy shit," he whispered.

"Yeah, my thoughts exactly." I closed my eyes and brought up a hand to cup his cheek. "So, maybe we sober up really quickly and do this?"

"I'm game." Kennedy nodded.

I paused the movie and headed to the kitchen to make coffee.

We needed coffee and we needed it *now*.

CHAPTER 8

KENNEDY

What the hell was I doing? I was very happily buzzed, definitely not wasted, but my intelligence had obviously escaped the basement and left me with idiotic ideas and raging hormones.

Suggesting Cody and I have sex just to "get it over with" was likely the dumbest thing I'd ever done. My past had taught me I was worthless and stupid in oh so many ways, but getting drunk with Cody and telling him we could fuck just to end our imprisonment was definitely the stupidest.

But, damn, the idea of touching him and feeling his body against mine was lodged in my fuzzy head, and I had no clue how to make the longing go away. I'd had plenty of impersonal hookups, so Cody and I could fuck each other's brains out, get out of our little basement situation, bitch out Jay for the next year or so, and maybe even end our little We Hate Each Other club.

Cody rummaged around on the small countertop, assembling the supplies for our coffee.

I grabbed onto his hips and pressed myself firmly against him, my chest colliding solidly with his thick, wide back. He froze, resting his hands on the counter and rocking his ass into me. We stayed in the arousing and awkward position while Cody finished the makings of coffee. When he hit the on button on the coffee maker, I soon found myself spun around and thrust firmly against the pantry door.

"We need to be sure about this," Cody growled.

"What's to be sure about?"

"One, I need to know you're not drunk." Cody's eyes were on fire as he glared down at me. I wasn't that much shorter than him, but our position forced me to look up at him.

"And two?" I teased, flicking out my tongue to lick the hollow where his neck and chest met.

"That we both agree this is consensual, random, and completely casual." Cody lifted his chin, giving me more access to his salty, musky neck.

"I'm not that drunk. And this is consensual, random, and completely casual." I repeated the requirements.

"Okay, coffee first, though. I don't want us rushing into something without giving ourselves time to mull it over." Cody moved away from me, turning back to the coffee.

"I never thought you'd be the type to think things over and make a common thing into such a big deal." I wandered over to the counter, joining Cody.

"Usually I'm not. This is just different. We know each other, we have mutual friends, we can't fuck and then never see each other again," Cody grumbled as he waited for the coffee.

"You do that a lot? Fuck strangers and then never see them again?" I wasn't sure why the thought bothered me. I'd had my fair share of random hookups that I likely wouldn't even recognize if I saw them on the street.

"Some." Cody shrugged. "It's a lot easier sometimes if it works out that way."

"Maybe." I returned the shrug. "But, it doesn't have to be a disaster if we don't let it be."

"True." Cody reached around me for two coffee mugs. "I guess part of me really doesn't want Jay's damn little plan to work."

"And the other part of you?" I pressed.

Cody turned and studied my face with intensity. "The other part of me? I don't know. Can I get back to you on that one?"

He said the words in joking tone, but I caught the seriousness in his eyes.

"Sure." I let him off the hook, because I wasn't sure if I wanted a deeper answer. "Where's my coffee? I either need more shots or coffee."

Cody laughed. "More shots is a definite no for the time being." He poured steaming liquid into my mug and handed it to me.

We headed back to the couch. Each of us took a seat on opposite ends, sitting on one leg tucked underneath and one leg hanging over the side. Sipping our coffee, eyeing each other over the top of our mugs, Cody and I settled into a sexy, comfortable, anticipatory silence and let the caffeine do its work as it coursed through our veins.

"So, tell me about the *real* Kennedy Marks," Cody began.

Immediately defensive, I shrugged. "Not much to tell. My parents were rotten. They died when I was ten. I lucked out with some great foster parents who eventually adopted me. But, my first ten years were the most formative and damning. I don't like to dwell much on the past."

"I'm sorry about your parents." Cody sipped his coffee.

"Don't be. Like I said, they were rotten." I had no plans of ruining what was already a sucky weekend with a woe is me story of how much my childhood fucked me up.

"What were your foster parents like?" Cody tried again.

"They were great. Took me a long time to accept they were good people and an even longer time to realize they truly loved me and wanted what was best for me." I still held a large amount of guilt for not appreciating my adoptive parents as much as I should have and much sooner than I did. "It's amazing they stuck with me and didn't give up."

"You still see them a lot? Have a good relationship with them?"

"Yeah, they don't live far away. They are good people, and I see them as often as I can." I smiled at the thought of Mom and Dad. "But, they are both retired and travel a lot these days."

"What were you like in school?" Cody prodded.

"No, enough about Kennedy." I turned the tables on him. "You are super close with your parents and sister, right?"

Cody narrowed his eyes, but took the bait. "Yeah, my parents and I are super close. And Sadie is great. The guys and I were older when my sister came along, so we were immediately protective. She gets tired of it sometimes, but I like to think she enjoys having her own little security team."

"You enjoy working with your parents?"

"For the most part, yes." Cody nodded. "Mom doesn't come into the restaurant much these days. She's usually off with Micah's mom volunteering or getting coffee or baking or doing crafts. But Dad is there almost as much as I am. He's even ventured into Leather Sundays a time or two just to be sure he knows what's going on in his establishment. But he knew from the beginning that I'd never put the business in danger. Leather Sundays have actually helped boost business. We get a lot of people coming in throughout the week, driving from nearby towns, just to eat or enjoy the atmosphere of the B & B because they've been to Leather Sundays."

"What's the toughest part of the restaurant business?" I sipped my coffee.

Cody thought for a moment. "Balancing everything I think. Keeping the kitchen running, the alcohol stocked and poured, the customers happy, the revenue coming in, the supplies stocked, the waiters and waitresses scheduled and satisfied. There's a lot to balance."

"I can see that." I agreed.

"What about the hardest part of police work?" Cody turned the conversation again.

"Not being able to fix everything," I answered immediately and honestly.

"Like what?"

"BJ is a pretty small town. We don't have tons of crime, but there's a lot of drugs and domestic abuse cases." I shook my head. "Watching kids get mixed up with drugs, watching families fall apart at the hands of meth, watching victims of domestic abuse suffer again and again yet not being able to convince them to leave, those are all things that are hard to deal with. I want to protect and save all the kids and keep them away from drugs. I want to wring the necks of the people making and using meth. The average every day citizens who are strung out on prescription pills." I took a deep breath. "The hardest is watching a spouse or partner stay with an abuser, especially if kids are involved."

"Yeah, I bet that's hard to see. Makes you wonder why they don't just leave." Cody drained his coffee and placed the mug on the table in front of the couch.

"A lot of the victims stay because the abuser threatens worse. Threatens to hurt the kids, threatens to take the money, tell lies about them, all sorts of shit to convince the victim that they are better off staying in the relationship rather than leaving." I gritted my teeth at the memories of my own family so very long ago.

"Yeah, but if children are involved, how can a parent put their kids through that?" Cody shook his head. "I just don't see how a mom or dad can keep their child in a dangerous and abusive situation."

"Sometimes I think the victim is so far gone, so damaged, so weak they don't have it in them to think about others. Or they think they are doing the best they can." I knew from the few decent memories I had of my mom that she really did think she could keep me safe from my father as long as she took the brunt of the abuse.

"Okay, best part of your job?" Cody switched the subject and for that I was grateful.

"Best part is helping people. I see most of my life as completely out of my control, but when I'm in that uniform and helping to enforce laws and keep people safe and make sure things are done right, I can actually feel like I've got some say in the situation." The words spilled out and I wanted to snatch them back, think them over, process them again and again. "Keeping a kid calm and safe when Mom has had a fender bender. Teaching a young kid the reasons why stealing is wrong. Properly preparing kids for safe hunting and boating. Assisting shop and business owners with catching the petty thieves that sometimes show up in BJ. I know I don't do a whole lot more than make sure people are doing more than a rolling stop at the four-way stop sign, but I like knowing that I'm helping to keep BJ safe and orderly and maybe giving people a better image of police officers than what they might have been exposed to before."

"You're very good at what you do. You do your job well in a small town, and I'm sure you'd do just as well in a large city. Do you ever think about transferring to someplace bigger than BJ?" Cody asked.

"Trying to get rid of me?" I chuckled and placed my coffee cup on the table. "No, I don't think a bigger city would be good for me. I like the sense of community, the sense of belonging, and the sense that I can maybe actually reach and help a few. I think in the big city I'd feel lost and hopeless and alone." I shrugged. "What about the best part of your job?"

A soft smile graced Cody's face. "All of it?" He laughed. "No, there are tough parts and parts I don't love. But, overall, I really like what I do. I love to interact with customers. I love introducing people to new foods and alcohol while still serving the same old comfort foods and time-tested drinks. I love being able to set my own hours, change up the menu if I want, and be part of a tight-knit community."

"Would you want to do the whole restaurant thing in the big city? Say head on up to Indianapolis and open up something newer, bigger, better?" I prodded.

"Nah, I don't think so. Restaurants are a dime a dozen in big cities. I like what the Parker name and family has established here in BJ. I'm not scared of a little competition, but I don't want to start over."

"What if you could already be completely established? Would you want to live and work in the big city?" I could see Cody fitting in perfectly in a metropolis setting.

"I don't know. I like going to the city, but I think I'd miss the slower pace of our small town. I'd miss the everybody knowing everybody else. Sometimes that isn't good, but I do think I'd miss it." Cody rubbed a hand through his hair.

"So," I hedged, unsure of whether we'd sobered up enough for Cody's liking and if we were still on the same page with our plans.

"You feel sober?" Cody asked.

"Definitely. I was losing the buzz before the coffee, but it's totally gone now." I ran my palms down my jeans.

"Can you walk a straight line, touch your fingers to your nose, and read me my rights?" Cody stood.

I stood and faced him. "Can you?" I took a step forward.

Cody chuckled at my challenge. "Walking the line and touching my nose, yes. Reading rights, nope."

I shouldered past him and walked a straight line, touching my fingers to my nose, and reciting Miranda Rights which were cemented into my brain so far I didn't even have to think about them. "Satisfied?" I turned toward him. "Your turn." I gestured with my hand.

Cody took his own trip down the imaginary line, one foot in front of the other, alternating fingertips to nose. "Good enough for you?"

I lifted a shoulder. Were we still planning to consummate things and bring the awkwardness to a whole new level? Sex had seemed like a great idea when I was drinking. But now? Was Cody Parker someone I wanted to get involved with?

"You need the bathroom?" Cody gestured toward the bathroom.

So, yeah, seemed like we were still doing it. "Um, sure. Sounds good."

Fifteen minutes later, I'd taken care of preparations thanks to Jay's bulk buying of enemas. I emerged from the bathroom to find Cody spread out on the bed, his jeans off, and a towel spread out on the bedspread.

"We still doing this?" Cody lifted his head from the bed

"I'm game if you are." I shucked my pants.

Cody rolled from the bed and took his own fifteen minutes in the bathroom while I got comfortable. When he returned, I watched him search the bedside table for condoms and lube before he crawled into bed with me.

"I'm not against wining and dining and flowers and romance, but are we in agreement that this isn't going to be that type of hookup?" Cody propped himself up on an elbow as he rolled to his side.

"Definitely, I don't need candlelight and sweet words or romance. I'm a sure thing." I rolled to face him.

Cody leaned in for a kiss, but I put a hand on his chest to stop him. "If we're keeping this casual and random, maybe we skip the kissing?" I knew the fire that had lit my insides from our previous kiss would rage higher and hotter if we engaged in it during a more intimate moment. And the less intimate, the better in this case.

"Yeah, sure." Cody agreed before pushing me to my back and lifting my shirt. His teeth grazed my nipples, first one then the other, and I wondered momentarily if Cody would enjoy nipple clamps. I knew they could bring a lot of pleasure.

But his mouth was already making its way down my torso. When he reached the jock, he snapped the band. "Take it off," he ordered.

"Only if you do." I nodded my head toward the colorful jock he wore.

Cody kept his eyes pinned on me as we both slid the material from our bodies to expose ready and willing cocks, bobbing against our bellies. Cody ripped off his own shirt before removing mine.

Hauling me up by my shoulders, he positioned my head at the foot of the bed and rolled me to my side before he positioned himself right at my ready and waiting cock. His hot breath tickled the hairs at the base of my dick. Gripping his own length in his fist, he slapped my face with it, "Suck it."

I opened wide and swallowed him down, moaning as his mouth engulfed my cock at the same time. As far as sixty-nine went, I decided this one was in the Top Ten. When Cody rolled to his back, taking me with him, and he let my cock loose so he could concentrate on rimming my ass, the moment graduated into the Top Five of all sixty-nines ever. A tiny voice in my head wondered how good it would be if we *were* allowing kissing and intimacy and romance. But, those things got messy, so it was better to keep it impersonal. Although, could I really call another guy tongue fucking my ass *less* intimate? Maybe just a different kind of intimate.

Cody slapped my ass. "Get on your hands and knees." The command sent a slight thrill through me, but a deeper shot of ecstasy zinged through my veins when I imagined *me* telling *Cody* to suck me, *me* eating *Cody's* ass, *me* telling *Cody* to get on his hands and knees.

Pushing aside the mental torture, I moved to my hands and knees. Doggy style was the position I adopted for most random fucking when I was of the mindset, *"Let's fuck and get this over with quick. I don't want to see your face."* And, although I had no issue with Cody's face, I believed the impersonality of the position suited our random fuck just fine.

"You need prepping?" Cody ran a hand over my ass as I imagined him in front of me on all fours.

"No, I'm good with just some lube." I heard Cody rip open the condom first and flip open the lube bottle next. Soon a cool liquid dribbled into my ass before Cody's finger rubbed it in and dipped quickly in and out of my hole.

"You good?" Cody asked from behind me, his cock prodding at my ass.

"Yep." I leaned down on my elbows and spread my knees to expose more of my ass.

The broad head of Cody's cock teased and taunted my hole until he finally pressed in with one quick thrust. My hands grabbed handfuls of the bedspread, my breath caught in my throat, and my inner muscles screamed at the invasion. Cody slowed to allow my body time to adjust before he began a deep and forceful rocking into my ass.

No words were spoken, no kisses or soft caresses exchanged, and no feelings crossed paths. It was just as we'd agreed upon. Random, casual, and meant nothing. When Cody's orgasm filled the condom, the liquid heat pulsing inside me, I gripped my cock and pumped hard to the rhythm of Cody's cock in my ass until I came all over the towel.

When Cody pulled slowly from my body and shuffled to the bathroom, I felt immediately bereft. Everything had gone as planned. The sex was good as far as random sex went. It was slightly less awkward because I knew Cody as a pseudo friend, and slightly more awkward for that exact same reason. I had no complaints.

Except.

Why did I feel like it was so much less than what it could have been?

We fit together well. We both got off. Our flushed skin, heavy breathing, and throbbing cocks were proof positive of good sex.

Except.

I wanted better.

I wanted more.

I wanted to dominate Cody, push him, challenge him, hurt him, and soothe him.

I wanted to own him.

CHAPTER 9

CODY

What the actual fuck had just happened?

Sex with Kennedy had been good. Really good.

But something was off. Something was missing.

Was it just because we'd kept things so impersonal?

Or?

I envisioned me on my back at the edge of the bed with Kennedy standing between my legs, bent over me to cup my face and kiss me as he thrust deeper and deeper into my body.

The mental fantasy switched to my body immobilized in a sling, held captive with leather straps and chains while Kennedy punished my ass with a flogger before soothing the pain with his tongue and lips. My balls were drawn tight, constricted by the cock ring, and I begged Kennedy to relieve the pressure from the clamps on my nipples.

I ripped the condom from my cock and yanked open the shower before the fantasies could go any further.

Kennedy and I had scratched an itch. Given in to something primal.

Damn if I'd admit we'd let Jay win.

But that was where it had to stop.

Kennedy Marks and Cody Parker did *not* belong together. If we were lucky, we'd be able to be civil to each other after this stupid weekend. But anything more was out of the question.

When I emerged from the bathroom twenty minutes later, pissed to still be wearing my day old jeans and another tank and jock, I eased back as Kennedy brushed passed me wrapped in the comforter.

"Just gonna shower real quick," he mumbled.

Well, now we could add awkward to our list of issues.

By the time Kennedy joined me on the couch, I'd grabbed the expensive beer from the fridge and had cold one waiting for him.

"We gonna talk?" I asked.

"What's to talk about? Sex is sex. It was good. End of story, right?" Kennedy downed at least half the bottle of beer before his gaze finally met mine.

"What're we sayin' to Jay and the guys?"

Kennedy shrugged. "Tell 'em we scratched the itch, things were good, and we'll try harder to get along when we're around them."

"Yeah, okay, sounds good." I finished my beer.

"Good beer, at least." Kennedy drained his and grabbed another just as I reached into the cooler.

Our hands brushed and the electric heat could have melted the ice.

"Yep, good beer. May as well enjoy." I agreed.

"You think they'll come check on us tonight?" Kennedy twisted the cap from his beer and took a swig.

"Doubt it. Little fucker said they were all going to cover Leather Sunday so I bet they won't come back until tomorrow night." Just thinking about the situation made me want to kill Jay all over again.

"Well, then I guess we drink beer, watch some movies, and enjoy the comfy bed." Kennedy shrugged again.

"You can have the bed," I began.

Kennedy rolled his eyes. "You just licked my ass, pretty sure we can sleep in the same bed without being any more awkward than this conversation has been."

I cringed but couldn't help the laugh that escaped. "Yeah, you got that right."

Kennedy and I spent the rest of our afternoon and evening eating frozen pizzas, finishing off the beer, and watching comedy movies.

"Dude, I'm zonked. I'm gonna crash." Kennedy stood and stretched.

I checked the clock on the television guide. It was past midnight. "Whoa, we wasted the entire day."

"Yeah, not sure the last time I ever did that. It was actually sort of nice." Kennedy shucked his jeans at the edge of the bed.

I willed my eyes not to stare at his ass all tight and perky in the jock.

"Part of me hates how much I missed at work and doing odds and ends that needed worked on, but it was kinda nice to just do nothing." I took my cue from Kennedy and stripped my pants too. Would he be fighting to keep his gaze from my ass?

When I turned toward the bed, Kennedy had climbed in and rolled to his side with his back to me. Guess he didn't have issues.

I crawled under the covers and turned my back toward him. The Grand Canyon of space between us was filled with enough tension to wrap around the earth at least twice.

How could I regret something so much yet not regret it in the least bit? So much for the control I thought I had on my life. One hot guy and one quick fuck and things turned to shit.

~~*

"Oh my god. It worked. Look at them. They look so in love and so happy. I bet they'll get married and have little butt babies within the next year." Jay's stage whisper woke me, and I immediately realized I was wrapped in the warm cocoon of Kennedy's arms.

I cracked an eye to see Jay decked out in a unicorn t-shirt and short shorts. The shirt said, *"I'm too beautiful to die."* Jay clasped his hands together in front of his chest and bounced on his toes. "Maybe they'll be so happy they won't want to kill me."

"I doubt that. Pretty sure they're still going to kill you." Micah laughed. "Even all curled up in

Kennedy's arms, Cody still looks pissed beyond belief. Look at that scowl."

I furrowed my brow deeper and moved Kennedy's arm from around my chest before sitting up to face the crew.

"I'm going to climb in my truck, drive home, and I better not see you fuckers for a few days at least. Don't come to Leather Sunday." I stood and reached for my pants. "I swear I'm not responsible for what I'm going to do to all of you if you come sticking your fucking noses where they don't belong. *Again*." I heard Kenney roll from the bed behind me as I pulled on my pants.

"Same goes for me. I'm on duty the next three nights. I'd prefer to not see you all for a while."

I turned and watched as Kennedy covered his beautiful ass with his jeans before I walked to the bathroom to take a leak. Walking past the guys, I shoulder bumped Jay and glared at Levi when he growled and pulled his man close to his side.

Kennedy followed me up the stairs and out the door leaving the other four alone in the basement.

"If I thought they didn't have their phones, I'd say we should lock them in for a while." I ran a hand over my face and glanced around at the cloudy day.

"You think they'll really leave us alone for a while?" Kennedy asked as we headed toward our vehicles.

"Hell no." I scowled. "Jay will be bugging us for details before the end of this day."

"That's what I figured." Kennedy nodded. "We stick to it was good, we got it out of our systems, and we're going to try to get along now?"

"That's the story, and we're sticking to it." I yanked open my truck door.

"Sounds good." Kennedy gave a short wave. "See ya around."

~~*

Less than twenty-four hours later, Jay was in my office at the restaurant, and I was willing him to spontaneously combust so he—and the headache I was fighting would go away.

"Seriously, Cody, you're being such a prude." Jay flopped down on the couch. "Just tell me if it was good. I mean, I saw you all cuddled up in bed so I can only assume you had sex. I don't need the dirty details, unless you *want* to share, but just tell me it was as fabulous as I knew it would be."

"It was fine. I'm not giving details. You got your wish. End of story." I scanned the rough draft of my new brunch menu. I still had a ton to figure out as far as costs and prices and functionality within the kitchen, but I was looking forward to the new endeavor.

"Arrhh, you're so infuriating!" Jay crossed his arms and pouted.

"Get over it. That's all you're getting." I glared across my desk. "Go fuck with Levi. Or better yet, go *fuck* Levi, and leave me alone. You're damn lucky

I haven't tried to kill you. I had detailed plans for murder and dismemberment. Having a member of law enforcement on my side would be a huge help. Plus, there are plenty of places on Blueridge Hill to hide body parts." I cocked a brow and gave Jay my meanest stare.

The kid at least had the decency to blush and look slightly worried. "Fine, fine. I'll leave. But, I feel like there should have been something more when you two finally hooked up." He waltzed out the door.

"You and me both, kid. You and me both," I mumbled as I studied the menu in my hands again without really seeing it.

"We got a problem." Kennedy dropped onto a barstool a week later after the lunch rush.

"Oh shit, you're pregnant?" I kept my face totally serious.

Kennedy rolled his eyes. "Shut up, fucker."

I tossed the bar towel into the wash bucket. "Hey, Dad, I'm taking a break. Let me know if it gets busy," I hollered to my father who was shootin' the shit with some buddies at the tables near the door.

Dad raised his hand in acknowledgement.

"Come on. We can talk in my office. I haven't sat down all fuckin' day." I turned and walked toward the back without waiting for Kennedy to follow.

I settled in behind my desk and gestured for Kennedy to take a seat on the couch.

He chose the chair instead.

I raised a brow. "You here on official police business?"

"Yeah, looks that way." Kennedy pursed his lips.

I sat back in the chair and waited for him to continue.

"You know that new lady in town? The one who moved in a few months ago? Lives at the corner of Elm and Sycamore across from Linda's hair place." Kennedy described a middle-aged woman I knew only by appearance and gossip around town.

"Yeah, don't know her name, but I hear she's pretty much been a bitch to anyone and everyone she's had contact with."

"Her name is Vicki Stringer," Kennedy continued. "Guess she moved here after a recent divorce. Seems pretty bitter about life in general. Not sure why she chose BJ, but she's stirring pots, shaking hornets' nests, and spreading trouble everywhere she goes."

"Okay, so how does that cause a problem for us?" I wasn't sure where Kennedy was going.

"She's making complaints about Leather Sundays and is threatening to start a petition to get the B & B shut down completely." Kennedy watched for my reaction.

CHAPTER 10

KENNEDY

I waited to see if Cody would explode.

He rolled his eyes and pushed back from his desk. "Never gonna happen."

"Oh, I'm pretty sure it's going to happen if *it* is the petition. Ms. Stringer seems hell bent on closing down Leather Sundays."

"No, what I mean is it doesn't matter if she starts a petition. Too many people in town enjoy Leather Sundays to sign. And those who don't participate aren't the type to side with a newcomer over a founding family." Cody shook his head. "Lady doesn't know what she's getting herself into."

"I'll keep you updated on Stringer's plans and actions." I stood to leave. "You gonna be helping with the Blue Jay stuff this week?" I had several days off and had promised Jay I'd help.

"Yeah, Jay talked me into manual labor. You?" Cody rounded his desk and met me at the door.

My body quivered when I felt the heat from Cody's body and I smelled his deep, sexy scent. Gritting my teeth against wanting to throw him against the wall and fuck him raw, I swallowed thickly and nodded. "Yep, I'll be there, too. Sounds like he's got some hands-on projects for us."

We walked to the front. I waved goodbye to Cody and the locals before heading back to the station. Knowing Cody was going to be at the Blue Jay each night that week added a strange and thrilling little pep to my step.

"I need my two best guys to hang the basketball goals. Please and thank you." Jay pointed at Cody and me before turning back to whatever project he was working on with Cole.

"Since when did we become your best guys?" Cody cocked his head to the side and waited on Jay to turn around.

Jay smiled over his shoulder. "Since you let me live." He paused. "And since you're both so very big and strong I thought hanging the goals would be a good job for you."

"What about your own big strong man?" I teased.

Jay looked across the room to where Levi was building a set of cabinets and shelves for the rec room. "Clearly my man is perfectly capable, but also otherwise occupied. Now, Cole and I are working on some details that require more brain than brawn, so if you two would be dears and just get started on the goals, I'd very much appreciate it." Jay blew a kiss before going back to what he and Cole were discussing.

"Did he just say we have more brawn than brains?" Cody furrowed his brow.

"I believe he did." I slapped Cody on the shoulder. "Come on. He's survived without us killing him this long. Let's not hurt him now. We can surely handle some basketball goals."

We walked to the area of the abandoned building that had been set up as the basketball court. Thanks to Cody's dad and his connections, the court had been laid. A shiny wax finish would be put on in the next few weeks.

"You ever installed basketball goals?" I stood with my hands on my hips and stared at the supplies and tools.

"On a couple garages." Cody shrugged and grabbed the instructions.

"I never took you for the type to read directions."

"And I never took you for the type who *could* read," Cody shot back with a smirk.

I narrowed my eyes. Why did I get so damn turned on when Cody pushed my buttons?

"So, based on the way the area is set up, the goals are going to have to be installed on the walls." Cody glanced at the wall in front of us then back to the instructions. "First things first, we measure where they need to be, find the studs, install the hardware, and then we hang the goals."

"If you say so." I held up my hands. "I'll do whatever you tell me."

"Is that what you say to all the boys?" Cody taunted.

"Shut up. Where do you want me?" I grabbed a pencil, the instructions, and a tape measure.

"You really want me to answer that?" Cody chuckled, but followed me to the wall. "We'll need a ladder." He moved the ladder from the corner to where we were working. "You go on up. 'Bout as close as you'll ever get to being on top of me." Cody's words seemed laced with challenge.

I gritted my teeth, willed the bubble of anger and desire to settle, and climbed up the ladder. "You look good down there." I handed the end of the tape measure to Cody and waited for him to secure it on the floor. "I'm going to mark where the directions tell me. But, you'll have to find the studs."

Cody snorted. "Have trouble finding the studs? I figured you'd have them lined up for that pretty ass of yours."

I ignored his comment and marked the points where the goal would need to hang. "Okay, your turn." I climbed down the ladder. "Where's the stud finder?"

Before I could turn around, Cody's front met my back. "Right here. Think I found one." His voice was soft and low right at my ear.

"Yeah, well, pretty sure your radar is off," I scoffed and willed the zing of desire rushing through me to calm the fuck down.

"Nah, I'm very seldom wrong about a hot piece of ass." Cody's breath teased against my ear.

I backed up and moved away from his touch. "What the hell? Just a piece of ass, huh?"

Cody looked taken aback. "Thought we were keeping it casual, fun, no strings?"

"You're right, we are. My bad." Anger, embarrassment, and irritation battled inside my head. Cody hadn't really done anything wrong. Just a bit of harmless flirting. It was better than our usual arguing or ignoring each other. So why did his comment rub me the wrong way?

"Sorry, I didn't mean to cause an issue." Cody glanced at me questioningly before locating the stud finder and marking the points where the hardware would need to go.

An hour later, we'd spoken maybe ten more words, but the goals were hung.

"So, um, again, I'm sorry about earlier. Thought we'd reached a point where we could play." Cody grumbled his apology.

Play. The word shot straight to my dick. *Oh how I'd love to play with Cody Parker.*

"We're good. Just hard adjusting to us not constantly being at each other's throats." I tossed the tools back in the toolbox. "So, back here tomorrow evening for the slave master to give us more work?"

Cody chuckled. "Yeah, I'm sure Jay will have something planned for his *best boys*."

~~*

The next evening I debated going to the Blue Jay. I wanted to help Jay. I liked working on projects I knew would help the community and kids in trouble. And I wanted to see Cody.

Wanting to see Cody was what almost kept me at home. Since when did I *want* to see Cody? When did his presence anywhere dictate whether or not I went?

Never. Damn, Cody Parker. He would not be the reason I backed out of helping Jay. So, I grabbed my keys and headed toward the Blue Jay.

The BJ was in an old abandoned warehouse type building. Not huge as far as warehouses went, but tons of room for what Jay was needing it for. *A lot* of work had been done to get the building ready over the past several months. Most of what was left to do now was finishing touches, finalizing plans, working on getting word out, that type of thing.

I pulled up to the BJ and hopped out of my car. Maybe I could convince Jay to have me work with Micah or Levi tonight. If I had to work with Cody, I couldn't guarantee I wouldn't punch him or throw him against the wall and fuck him until he couldn't walk.

Damn it. Maybe we should go back to hating each other.

"There's my right hand man. Can't get my work done without my little partner." Cody's words boomed across the warehouse and his teasing grin dared me to react to his words. Was he purposely pissing me off? Never would have guessed he had a masochistic side.

I flipped him the bird and headed toward Jay.

"Yay, you're here. I need you and Cody to change all the burned out lightbulbs. Make sure every single light fixture works. We're going to have the final inspections and all that jazz soon, so I need everything in working order." Jay marked things off a list as he spoke.

"Cody can handle light bulbs. What else you got?"

Jay glanced up and narrowed his eyes. A slight evil grin teased his lips. "Why? Is being around Cody getting to you? Finding out maybe scratching that itch just once wasn't enough to soothe the flames? Finding out that there's a *very* fine line between hate and love?"

"Whoa, slow down there." I held up my hands. "Fine, I'll do lights. No problem." I turned to walk away.

"I'm just sayin," Jay started. "You guys have known each other for several years. Yeah, you've been at each other's throats for all of that time. But, turning the tables on that hate may bring about other strong emotions. Don't discount what you're feeling." Jay waggled his fingers, waving me away.

I did my best to ignore Jay's words and found Cody in the kitchen area.

"Ready to bring light unto the world?" Cody asked from his position on the ladder. His ass was right at eye level. That gorgeous, sexy-as-sin, bubble butt. I wanted to grab his ass cheeks, spread them wide, and bury my face and tongue in his body.

"Earth to Kennedy," Cody called from the ladder, staring at me over his shoulder. "You okay? You look weird."

Just thinking of all the dirty things I'd like to do to your ass. No biggie. The words ran through my head, and I coughed to cover the urge to laugh. "Huh? Yeah, I'm good. Let's get to it."

Cody finished the light then we headed to the hallway where several of the overhead lights were burned out.

Ten minutes later, my frustration level was through the roof. "Damn, man. You can't take directions worth shit."

"What the fuck does that mean?" Cody shot back from the top of the ladder. "Got the light changed, didn't I?"

I shook my head and snorted. "You ignored every suggestion I made, muscled in the bulb instead of doing it the right way, and refused my help which wasted at least five minutes. You suck at following orders."

Cody pinned me with narrowed eyes as he climbed slowly down the ladder. He jabbed at my chest with a finger. "First of all, I got the damn light changed. Nothing broken, no harm no foul. Second, I can take direction just fine when I choose to."

"Sure you can." I headed toward the next light a few feet down the hallway. "You're in charge at the restaurant. You're in charge of Leather Sundays. You're a big brother. You seem to run the show most of the time when it comes to you and Micah and Levi. When have you *ever* taken orders well? Or taken them at all?"

Cody was right in my face as soon as I turned around. "Damn straight, I'm in charge. I give the orders. I don't *need* anyone controlling me."

"What the fuck does that have to do with anything? I wasn't trying to control you. I was telling you how to change a lightbulb."

"Who put you in charge?" Cody growled. "No one. When and if I ever find myself needing or wanting to take orders from someone I'll let you know. Until then, fuck off."

Cody retreated down the hallway, shoulders tight, anger evident in his walk.

The only thing my fucked up mind could think about was that fuckin' gorgeous ass and all the nasty things I wanted to do to it. Mouthy, grouchy, pissing-me-off-to-no-end Cody was hot as sin and just asking for me to punish him.

No other man had ever stirred these feelings in me. Why Cody? Why the most dominant man I'd ever met? Maybe *I* was the masochist bringing the pain upon myself.

~~*

The following evening was the last night for Cody and me to help Jay with the BJ for a while. I had some shifts coming up, and Cody was busy implementing the new brunch menu at the B & B.

Thank the good Lord above, because I wasn't sure how much more "togetherness" Cody and I could take before a good old-fashioned blow up occurred.

The man seemed to be holding onto his bossy, arrogant, I'm-in-charge attitude with a very tight hand. Cody definitely didn't like even the inkling of giving up control or someone ordering him around.

And I was growing more and more positive that I wanted to get him in a harness, a cock ring, some nipple clamps, and a ball gag. I imagined him chained to my bed, me whipping him until he begged me to stop, and then me punishing every single inch of his goddamn beautiful body before I gave his ass the hard fucking it deserved.

Which was the crux of the problem.

I wanted to own Cody.

But Cody owned himself and others.

He belonged to no one.

But my fantasy had taken on a mind of its own, and there was no turning back.

And that was why I needed some space between us. I was happy to be helping Jay, but I needed a break from Cody before I exploded.

"Would you two be willing to work on the shelving units in the pantry area?" Jay gestured toward the large walk-in pantry where an array of loose premade materials and sheets of directions lay scattered across the floor.

"What happened to them?" Cody scowled.

Jay blushed and braced a fist on his popped hip. "I *may* have attempted to build them myself and got a little in over my head."

Cody and I glanced between the mess and Jay before busting out in laughter.

"What can I say? My creativity is *not* in construction." Jay sashayed toward the dance studio that was nearing completion at the end of the hallway.

"Guess we're building shelves." Cody headed toward the pantry.

I followed. "This is the biggest damn pantry I've ever seen." I marveled aloud.

"Yeah, I think it was the previous business's break room. But, since it's right next to the kitchen and dining room, it makes a great walk-in pantry. Most of the food will be canned, boxed, or dry goods, so a large area like this is perfect." Cody knelt and began to sort the pieces. "Damn, I think he's got two units all tossed together here."

An hour later, we'd sorted the shelving units into all the separate materials.

"Work separately and get the two done at once? Or work together and do one unit at a time?" I stood with my hands on my hips and waited for Cody to decide.

"As much as I'd love to put you to shame in building my unit quicker and better, it would probably be better to have two sets of hands per unit. So let's work together." Cody smirked.

"Whatever, I put together most of the furniture in my house, so I doubt you'd put me to shame." I rolled my eyes and glanced around. "Let's do the L shaped one first. It's probably going to be more difficult just due to size."

By the time the larger of the two shelving units was put together, I had almost ground my teeth to the gums trying not to blow up at Cody's bossy ass and arrogant attitude. And I'd been thinking of absolutely *anything* that would help to avoid my dick sporting wood. As much as Cody drove me insane, he also revved my engine like no man before.

"Come on. Let's get this other fucker together. I'm ready to get out of here." I headed toward the second unit.

"You getting crabby? A little physical labor too much for you to bear?" Cody teased and prodded.

I swore the glimmer shining in his eyes and the challenging grin on his lips were a sign the fucker was pissing me off on purpose and loving every single moment of it.

"Whatever. Let's just get started." I grabbed the directions and started moving the main pieces into position. "You plan on helping any or you just going to boss me around?"

"Thought you liked being bossed around?" Cody moved closer and bumped me with his elbow.

"Not by the likes of you."

Cody laughed. "Fine, let's finish this."

We worked in relative silence for about twenty minutes. Soon the last screw was twisted into place and the units positioned against the walls.

"'Bout time," I groused and headed toward the closed pantry door.

Cody reached an arm around my body and blocked the door. "What's up with you? You've always been able to get on my nerves, but you also used to be ready to go round and round with me. But, ever since our imprisonment, you've been different."

"And you haven't been?" I kept my back to him and gritted my teeth as the warmth of his body heated the air around me.

"Me? I haven't changed at all. It was a decent fuck, maybe not the best either of us have ever had, but I'm able and willing to move past it and try to put our hatred toward each other on the back burner."

Cody moved even closer to me, his breath warm at my ear. "I just don't understand why you've got to be such a pain in the ass."

I whipped around. "Stop being such an asshole," I growled.

"Yeah? Gonna make me?" Cody challenged.

"Someone needs to." I stepped forward, and my chest almost touched Cody. "Someone needs to take you over their knee and spank you until you admit you're not so big and strong and in control."

Cody's nostrils flared, and I feared I'd pushed him too far. "You think it could be you?" Cody's dare was a heated whisper as he gazed down at me.

Without a second thought, I grabbed Cody's shirt in two big fistfuls and spun him around. Pressing him solidly against the door, I pinned his hips with mine. "I'd take that challenge any day." Our breaths came quickly, the beating of our hearts pounding between our flush chests. My lips traced up his jawline until I reached his ear. "I promise I'd top you so hard, you'd never be the same."

"Prove it." Cody whispered and then stared at me, waiting for my next move.

Shock and desire shot through me. Did Cody *want* me to take control? Was he daring me only in this moment or was he talking about the bigger picture.

Giving no more thought to the questions bombarding my mind, I attacked Cody's mouth in a fierce kiss. The moment our lips met, a change took place between us. Cody gave in, let me control the speed and depth and the aggression of the kiss. And my desire to own him, body and soul, grew tenfold.

CHAPTER 11

CODY

Never had I let a kiss consume me.

Never had I let a man control me.

Never had I wanted to give up everything and do whatever another man demanded.

But for Kennedy, I would.

With Kennedy, it was what my heart and body longed for.

He owned me with that kiss, and I never wanted to lose the feeling.

My entire life, I'd been in control of absolutely everything. It was my strength, my safety, my security. But, in Kennedy's arms, his mouth ravishing mine, his body hard against my own, I let it all go. Kennedy's kiss promised pain and punishment as he nipped at my lip and raised my arms over my head to pin them against the door. But, within moments, his tongue soothed the sting of the bite, and I knew his kiss also promised thrilling ecstasy the likes of which I'd never experienced. If only I would give him that control. Let him own me. Submit to him.

A knock on the door shattered our moment. Jumping apart, wiping the taste of each other from our lips, and breathing as if we'd just run a marathon, Kennedy and I could only stare. His gaze seemed to mirror mine: wild, fiery, questioning, unsure of so much, yet solid in the realization that *something* huge had just taken place.

"You guys 'bout done?" Jay hollered from the other side of the door. "Ohhh, are you naked and getting nasty in there? I mean, once we open, I think that will be against Blue Jay policy. Not good around the children, ya know? But, if you're in there fuckin' each other's brains out for a second time, I think I could die happily right now."

Kennedy and I each chuckled and attempted to compose ourselves by running hands through our hair, straightening our clothes, and taking deep breaths. I eyed Kennedy and jerked my head toward the door.

He nodded.

I opened the door. "Sorry, we had to close it to get the units into place." This was the truth. Just not the reason we'd *kept* the door closed. Jay was way too damn intuitional when it came to Kennedy and me.

"Mmhm, sure," Jay snarked as he pushed past me and into the pantry. The younger man ran his gaze over Kennedy and me, narrowing his eyes. "You both seem flushed, heavy breathing, sparkly eyes." Jay glanced around. "But, you got way too much work done to have had time for conjugal activities. Fine, I guess you weren't bumping uglies and making butt babies."

Kennedy and I could only snort and roll our eyes.

"But, for the record, as long as the fornication doesn't occur in my place of business where we will be molding and shaping young minds, offering solace, and helping to heal the damaged, I am all for any type of activities you two decide to partake in." Jay walked around the pantry to study the shelves. "These look really great, guys. Thank you."

Jay's quick change of subject was enough to give my already spinning mind severe whiplash. "Glad you like them." I cleared my throat. "Listen, um, I need to head out. Got some work to do at the restaurant."

I wanted to throw Jay out of the pantry and drop to my knees for Kennedy right that second. But I also found myself scared to death of all that had transpired in the last twenty minutes. I needed to get away. Needed to think. Needed to be away from Kennedy.

Without a glance backward, I gave a quick wave of my hand to both Kennedy and Jay and all but ran from the Blue Jay. For the next several hours, I locked myself in my office at the B & B and lost myself in paperwork. Numbers, bottom lines, expenses, profits. I could work them, master them, and control them. But once I was home in my bed, my skin still damp from the scalding hot shower I'd taken in hopes of calming my head, I found myself unable to think of anything but Kennedy.

Kennedy taking charge.

Kennedy slamming me against the wall and devouring my mouth.

Promising to top me so hard.

My dick sprang to life once again as Kennedy's words played through my head on repeat.

"I promise I'd top you so hard, you'd never be the same."

No one had ever said that to me. Yes, had bottomed before, but only with toys and fingers, never full on penetration. *Wanting* to bottom, longing for a man to top me, control me, and own me. That was new territory. And it was confusing, frustrating, and hot as fuck all at the same time.

I fell into a fitful sleep wondering if Kennedy was having the same thoughts alone in his bed.

~~*

The weekday lunch rush was in full swing when Kennedy walked into the B & B. Used to be I bristled when I saw the man because he pissed me off so much. Now, while it still pissed me off, the bristling was more a sensation of butterflies in my stomach as I anticipated whatever words we might speak, whatever glances we might share, and whatever touches might pass between us.

Jesus fuck, what the hell was wrong with me? Cody Parker didn't get butterflies in his stomach over a guy. I needed a good fuck with a sub bottom, and I needed it now.

But what I got was a grinning Kennedy giving me a quick wave as he settled himself at the bar. So much for fucking the thought of him out of my system. The man was under my skin, in my head, and, if I wasn't careful, I was going to spend the rest of the lunch serving food with a massive hard-on tenting my pants.

Fuck.

I signaled to Dad real quick that I was heading to the back. I knew Dad and the other staff could handle the crowd, and I wouldn't be gone long. I just needed to get myself under control. I nodded to Kennedy and made my way to the office.

I stood in the middle of the room, hands on my head, eyes closed, and taking deep breaths. I needed to get a handle on my dick and get back out there. I wasn't the type to react so strongly to the presence of a man. *Any* man. Especially not Kennedy.

A knock at the door startled me from my thoughts.

"Yeah?" I knew I needed to get back to the floor to help finish with the rush.

Kennedy poked his head around the door. "You okay?"

The words jabbed at me. On one hand, they pissed me off. *Of course I was okay. Who was he to think he needed to check on me?* On the other hand,

I was touched and all aflutter that Kennedy would want to make sure I was okay. "I'm fine." I bit out.

He swung the door wide, slammed it behind him, and stalked toward me. He whispered, "Good" right before he gripped my face and kissed me like a starving man partaking in his first meal. Kennedy backed me toward my desk. When my thighs bumped into it, I sat and opened my legs.

"I can't stop thinking about you. About whatever the hell that was at the BJ." Kennedy spoke breathlessly against my lips between kisses.

"It was nothing," I muttered.

"You can keep telling yourself that all you want, but you and I both know it was definitely something." Kennedy ran his tongue along my bottom lip. "I can't say I completely understand it. Yet. But I definitely have an interest in exploring it a bit more."

I was silent and gave myself over to his demanding kiss. When had I ever let a man's kiss overtake me this way? Allowing Kennedy to lead was scary as fuck and refreshing and breathtaking all at the same time.

"You up for that?" Kennedy's question caught me off guard.

"For what?"

"For exploring whatever this might be." Kennedy backed away a bit, the question hanging between us.

I had no words, no coherent thoughts to share. I only knew I felt a longing deep in the pit of my stomach.

I nodded.

Kennedy smiled. Then kissed me again. "How about a date? Start slow, get to know each other better, and then we see where things head?"

I could only nod again. I didn't do much dating. Hookups, play and kink, fucking? Yes. Dates? Not so much. But, if Kennedy wanted a date, I would give him a date.

And since when did I care if a guy wanted a date?

Fuck me, I was screwed.

"Okay. I'll plan it all. I'll pick you up Friday night at six." Kennedy's statement left no room for argument. And I'll be damned if it didn't turn me on. My gut reaction was to tell him to stuff it and stop telling me what to do, but the little quivers traveling through my body at his simple demand told me I should just shut up and let the man make the plans.

Friday at six, I paced the porch, glancing at my phone to check the time, rethinking my choice in clothing about a million times, and convincing myself that Kennedy wasn't going to show up. Which was ridiculous. It was all ridiculous. I didn't wait and pace for a date. I didn't question my clothing. Jeans that hugged my ass, a fitted black t-shirt, and black leather boots were me. I didn't change that for anyone. I didn't worry that a man would stand me up. Others may have done all of that over *me*, but I wasn't one to obsess and tamp down nerves.

Until Kennedy Marks.

It was a damn date, not a marriage proposal.

The thought was meant to calm my mind, but it went straight to my gut. Marriage? I saw what Micah and Cole had, how happy they were. Levi and Jay were likely well on their way to a happily ever after. Did I want that? A lifetime commitment? Someone to love the rest of my life?

Fuck.

Couple years ago, I would have said I wasn't ready for that, wasn't looking, and marriage wasn't on my radar. Hell, a committed relationship wasn't even on my mind.

But, now?

Kennedy Marks had tossed my world upside down and brought a chaos that I had no clue how to deal with. But, if I was being honest with myself, I reveled in the way Kennedy made me feel, even if it wasn't my normal.

Maybe it was my new normal.

"And maybe you're being a big pansy-ass being worried about a date." I ran my hands through my hair as I mumbled, "It's just a date. No proclamations of love and commitment."

Kennedy saved me from myself by pulling up the drive a few moments later. He smiled as he emerged from the vehicle and walked toward the porch. "Sorry I'm late. Got stuck by a train."

"Likely story," I teased. Living in a railroad town meant getting stopped at the tracks more often than not. But, it was also a built-in excuse. However, the look in Kennedy's eyes as he gave me a once over made me instantly believe him. I felt as if he was admiring a piece of artwork. "Like what you see?" I huffed and started down the steps to meet him.

"Very much," Kennedy growled as he grabbed me around the waist and pulled me in close for a kiss. "You look amazing. So damn sexy." His mouth hovered over mine as he spoke, his breath warm and minty, before he closed the space to greet my lips with his.

When I came up for air, my head and goofy grin attempted to float away, but I grabbed them back like a damn child holding onto a balloon. Kennedy had me off-kilter more than I'd ever been in my entire life. "You look pretty damn great yourself." He did. I loved seeing him in his uniform, but the dark wash jeans and fitted button-up dark gray shirt with boots was also a look I'd never tire of seeing on him.

Kennedy blushed and turned toward the passenger side of the car. Part of me wanted to pout and stomp my foot, swearing I didn't need him to open my damn car door. The other part swooned. While it was true I may not *need* him to open my door, I knew it was a perfectly gentlemanly gesture and, quite honestly, stole my breath away.

"Thanks," I whispered as I climbed into the car.

When Kennedy was seated and buckled in, I glanced his way. "Where we going?"

"You ever just sit back and enjoy the ride and let someone else take care of you?" Kennedy smirked.

"No," I answered immediately and honestly.

"Well, you should learn to let go and just relax. We're going to dinner and something else after." Kennedy turned the car to head down Blueridge Hill.

"Something else? Gee, thanks for the details." I didn't like not knowing what was going on, but the look of pleasure and glee on Kennedy's face over having a little surprise suddenly seemed worth letting go of control for a bit. "Can you at least tell me where we're eating dinner?" As a restaurant owner, I was slightly discerning over eating establishments.

"That Japanese grill and sushi bar over in Stockton." Kennedy glanced my way. "If that meets with your distinguished pallet?"

I smirked. "It's not that I'm so *distinguished*, I'm just used to running my own place, so I have a hard time enjoying other places because my mind is constantly evaluating their layout, the menu, the staff, the food, and the presentation. I know the B & B is just a bar and grill, but I have a lot of pride in feeding people the meals they desire and knowing the food will be the best it can be."

"You run an amazing restaurant and people love it." Kennedy reached over and placed his hand on my thigh.

Heat shot directly to my groin.

"But, tonight, let's just stuff ourselves with meat and sushi and not worry about the entrepreneur side of things."

I smiled and savored the heat of Kennedy's hand on my leg. "I'll try."

Stockton was about forty-five minutes away. Our table was ready when we arrived. I wasn't used to the warm and gushy feelings in my chest at the thought of Kennedy planning the whole night just for us. I'd never been *wined and dined*, but it appeared I enjoyed it. *Huh, who knew?*

A smiling waitress led us to a very secluded back corner of the restaurant. She placed the menus on the table and waited for us to scoot into the round booth. The table and booth were circular, and we ended up shimmying to the middle and sitting much closer than was likely necessary. But, the warmth of Kennedy's thigh against mine secured me to that spot without question.

"To drink?"

"I'll have water, please." I ordered as I began to peruse the menu.

"Water. And we'll both have sake, please."

Kennedy ordering the Japanese rice wine for me should have pissed me off. But it didn't. *What the hell was going on?*

"You want the sushi bar and grill? Or order from the menu?" Our waitress asked with pen poised to write down our requests.

"You wanna just get the bar and grill?" Kennedy asked me without taking his eyes from the menu.

"Eh, I've never ordered sushi. I wouldn't know what to get." Sushi seemed like one of those fun things that you needed an expert to help you try for the first time.

"If I help you order what you'd like, will you try it?" Kennedy bumped my shoulder.

Not wanting to make our waitress stand there much longer, I agreed.

"Go on up. Plates are at the bar. Tell them what you'd like." The girl left to get our drinks.

We returned to the table with plates heaped high with grilled steak, chicken, and shrimp. Our waitress followed shortly with our gigantic order of sushi. Vegetable roll, Western roll, Volcano roll, and Dynamite roll. Kennedy promised I'd love them all. I was skeptical, but looking forward to trying the new food.

"How are we going to eat all of this?" I gazed at our table packed full of food.

"We can take some home if needed. I actually brought a cold bag with an ice pack if we need to keep things cold." Kennedy spoke as he began plating our food. "Better question, how have you gone this long without trying sushi?"

I shrugged. "Never knew what to order."

"Didn't want to look like you didn't know what you were doing?" Kennedy cocked a brow.

"Maybe," I murmured and reached for the plate he held out. The meat smelled delicious, and the sushi looked great. I glanced around for a fork.

"Try the chopsticks first. If they don't work, we'll ask for forks." Kennedy held up his chopsticks and winked.

After several attempts at picking up the meat, I started to get the hang of it. "Well, I guess I wouldn't starve if I was required to use them."

"Okay, we'll start with the easy one. Vegetable roll. Here, try it." Kennedy held a sushi roll on chopsticks and moved it toward my mouth.

My gut reaction was to balk at the action as too intimate and demeaning. I was a grown man. I could feed my damn self. But, the fire in Kennedy's eyes stopped me. Raising a brow, I pushed away the feeling and opened my mouth. I chewed, I savored, and I knew immediately I'd found a new favorite. "Even if I don't like the others, I think I could eat that the rest of my life and be happy." I washed the vegetable roll down with water.

As if living in an alternate universe, Kennedy and I spent the next twenty minutes feeding each other bites of sushi from chopsticks and sipping sake. I wasn't sure if I'd *ever* had a more enjoyable dining experience.

"So, you like sushi now?"

"If I get to eat it like this every time? Definitely." I reached over and thumbed away a piece of rice stuck on Kennedy's lip. When he leaned his cheek against my hand, I did what seemed to be the most natural thing in the world. I cupped his face and pulled him close for a soft, warm kiss. "Thank you for dinner."

Kennedy returned the kiss. "You're welcome."

"Now will you tell me what's next?"

"No," Kennedy teased.

I huffed. "You're lucky I like you, you know?"

Kennedy paused in pulling out his wallet. "I know I am. Truly. Liking each other is proving to be a whole hell of a lot more fun than hating each other."

"Yeah, I hear ya." I frowned. "Wonder why we spent so long with the hate?"

"Maybe we just weren't ready for this until now." Kennedy handed the bill and his card to the waitress as he spoke. "But, I plan on enjoying the change."

"Agreed." I finished my sake and water.

We left the restaurant and headed to who the hell knew where. I did my best to settle in and enjoy the evening.

Having Kennedy's hand in mine helped.

CHAPTER 12

KENNEDY

I knew I was taking a chance. The date, the meal, and the after dinner plans—all of it was a risk. Taking Cody out of his element and away from his control could backfire in the worst of ways.

But instead, I found Cody attempting to relax and go along with the spontaneity and letting me call the shots. I also found that a compliant Cody, willing to let me lead, was hot as fuck and went straight to my head. Never in my life had I wanted so badly to lead, to control, and to care for someone. Never had I thought anyone would want that from me.

And yet, I'd set the ball in motion, and I was quickly learning that perhaps I'd never wanted to control or care for or make the decisions because it hadn't ever been the right man. I wanted to talk to Cody about the whole situation, but I wasn't sure either of us were ready for that. Yet.

So instead, I enjoyed watching Cody's face try to figure out what the hell we were doing when I pulled the car up to an indoor water park.

"Um, pretty sure this place is closed." Cody sounded like he felt bad for me.

"It is." I climbed from the car and grabbed a duffle bag from the back. "Come on."

Cody left the car and fell into step beside me. "If it's closed, what are we doing? I know an officer of the law isn't going to perform a breaking and entering."

"Maybe this officer knows the owner. Maybe the owner gave the officer the key. Maybe we have the entire evening to swim and slide until our hearts are content." I winked as I pushed the key into the back entrance Mark had told me to use. Warm, moist, chlorine laden air blasted me upon entry.

"I didn't bring trunks," Cody began.

"No worries, I brought you some." I held up the duffle bag. "Come on. Let's change. I haven't been on slides like this since I was a kid. I plan to wear myself out before we leave."

In the locker room, hanging our clothes up on the towel hooks and changing into swim trunks, Cody inquired about the place again. "Seriously, though, who owns this place?"

"Being friends with an officer of the law has it perks." I waggled my brow. "Honestly, though, he's the son of friends of my parents. He shuts the business down during the colder months of the school year, actually only opens it on Winter Break, so he said we could use it tonight."

"Your real parents?" Cody winced. "Sorry, that sounded bad."

"Don't sweat it. My biological parents had no friends, at least not that I could tell. Mark is the son of my adoptive parents' friends. Anytime you hear me talk about *my parents* in a positive way, you can always assume I'm talking about the ones who adopted me. Always."

"Maybe you can bring them to BJ some day? Lunch at the B & B is on the house." Cody winked.

"They'd like that. They are really good people." I reached for towels and tossed one to Cody. "They got me at a really difficult time and it only got worse as I entered the teen years. I feel bad that I was so much trouble for them."

"I doubt they look at it that way." Cody cocked his head. "I bet they are super proud of their son."

Heat pinked my cheeks and I squirmed under the compliment.

"I'm not going to rest until you realize compliments are true and you're worthy of them." Cody snapped the towel at me as we both laughed. "How were your parents when you came out?"

"Pretty much fine. I think they were just relieved I was speaking to them. They were worried what it would mean for me. They knew I already dealt with a lot of self-doubt and feelings of worthlessness, so they were concerned how I would handle negativity from society. But, mostly, they were totally fine with it." I snapped my towel back at Cody. "Come on, time's a wastin'!"

Never in the history of man and water slides had two grown men had so much fun racing down steep watery inclines. Was it the adrenaline? The company being shared? Or the fact that each slide race ended with Cody and I wrestling at the bottom in the landing pool? Arms and legs wrapping and writhing, chests bumping, and finally hot, wet mouths meeting.

"Let's do the big one. Two people can go down at once." Cody whispered against my mouth.

"Two people going down at once sounds like last weekend at Leather Sunday," I teased and we both laughed.

When we reached the top of the wider, double-rider slide, we had to decide positioning. As much as I wanted to wrap my arms around Cody and hold him tight, I realized his taller and bulkier frame needed to be in the back. We got situated with me sitting between his legs, and my back against his chest. One of the best parts of being in the water slide complex completely alone was we had no one watching, no one waiting, and nothing stopping us from whatever we wanted to do.

"Hey," Cody spoke at my ear, and I turned to look at him.

"Yeah?" My word was breathy and my trunks were getting tight. I could feel Cody's similar reaction at my lower back.

Cody leaned down and kissed me, his arms wrapped under mine and holding tight around my chest. Water splashed and rippled as our lips and tongues mated and danced. Cody's thumb teased my nipple and I groaned. There was no role expectation or role reversal in the kiss. We were simply two men, attracted to each other, enjoying our time together and partaking in the pleasure of our bodies.

"Good thing we're alone. If kids were here, we'd definitely be in trouble for indecency." Cody murmured in my ear as he reached for my hard cock and stroked it as he thrust his own hard length against my backside.

"Yeah, definitely a place to avoid when children are around." I agreed and let my head fall back on Cody's chest as he stroked me.

"Can you imagine how much fun this would be with all the BJ Boys?" Cody chuckled. "My God, even if you can't get this place for free again, we should ask Mark if we can rent it out for just the six of us some evening."

"That would be so much fun."

"You ready?" Cody repositioned me in his arms so we were seated more upright.

The thrill of being in Cody's arms, rushing down a twisting and turning water slide, and splashing into the pool at the bottom added to the desire and heat already coursing through my body was enough to send me floating on Cloud Nine for the rest of the night.

Cody and I swam to the edge of the landing pool. "Lazy river?" I pointed to the river that circled around the complex.

"Yeah, but let's get one of those huge tubes so we can both lay on it." Cody pulled himself from the pool and headed to get the tube from the ultra slide.

"Do you think it will even fit?" I laughed as I followed him.

"Guess we'll see. Another perk to being here by ourselves. No rules to follow." Cody grabbed the giant tube made for eight riders and walked to the edge of the lazy river to toss it in. "Bingo! Perfect fit." He jumped into the water and climbed onto the tube. Holding his hand out to me, Cody smiled. "Would you care for a river raft ride on this fine evening, sir?"

"Permission to come aboard?" I teased.

"Granted, of course." Cody grasped my hand and hauled me onto the tube.

Because of the ride the tube was made for, there was a bottom, so we were sitting in a boat-like float. The gentle current of the river pushing us along.

Cody situated himself with his back to the outer edge of the ring and patted the space next to him. "Hopefully we won't unbalance ourselves." He mocked a worried look.

I shimmied over to sit next to him. The opposite side of the tube did come up from the water a bit, but we stayed afloat.

"So, while I'd very much love to do more than making out on the river, I feel it a bit inappropriate to do anything sexual where cameras could be watching and where children will be playing the next time this place opens." Cody rattled off his concerns.

"Agreed, completely." I chuckled. "I think some kisses are about as far as we need to go."

"Oh, but the fun we can have with those kisses." Cody tightened his arm around me and turned to bring my face to his.

"And, the kisses can be the preshow entertainment until we're somewhere with no cameras and no minors partaking of the same activities." I kissed him, gently at first and then gripping his hair in my fists to take control of the kiss.

Cody broke the kiss long enough to growl, "I like the sound of that." Then he allowed me to commandeer the kiss again.

I straddled his waist and continued to kiss him.

"Would you really want to top me? Dominate me?" Cody pushed me away for a second with his question.

I paused and gazed down at his heaving chest and his puffy lips. "In a split second, no question. As long as you were on board with it."

"Why? I thought you were into subbing and bottoming?" Cody cocked his head.

"Have been, always. I've topped a few guys, but only because they were steadfast bottoms. But, bottoming has always been where I naturally landed in any kind of hookups or even short relationships. I'm not the controlling type. I don't give orders. I don't take the lead or call the shots." I rocked my ass on his cock.

"But with me?" Cody grabbed my waist and thrust up against me.

"With you? I don't know. It's all I can think of. I know I'm not big and tough and strong enough either physically or emotionally to top any guy, especially you, but it's what my body and mind want." I lowered my chin to my chest, feeling embarrassed and waiting for Cody to laugh at me.

He chucked my chin up with his fist. "Don't. Don't do that. You have every right to your thoughts and feelings. Don't ever look ashamed for them." He leaned up to kiss me. "I gotta tell you, us switching from hating each other to whatever this non-hating-each-other thing is has me in a bit of a tailspin, and I can't really make heads or tails of my thoughts and feelings."

"It's okay. I don't expect you to ever want to bottom or submit to me. Look at you," I started and gestured toward his broad, hairy chest. "And, really, who am I to turn down bottoming for *this*?"

"Would you shut up for a second?" Cody grabbed my hands. "What I was *trying* to say is that I've never really thought about bottoming or subbing. Everyone has always just assumed I'm a top. And, I have always played the part of dominant very well in bed. I've always enjoyed it. No complaints."

"But?"

"But then something put the seed in my head of being under you and my whole world tipped on its axis, and I've not been able to think of anything else ever since." Cody said the words with a glint of challenge in his eyes as he stared into mine.

I let his words sink in for a moment. "So, you'd be willing to bottom for me? Maybe even sub if we played?"

Cody was silent for a few beats. "Ready, willing, and able on the bottoming. And looking forward to whatever leather play you can think up for us. I sort of know a guy who could probably hook us up." He chuckled.

My heart and head swam with thoughts and plans and possibilities. "I've always been the one in the harness, ball gag, and clamps while getting my ass flogged. The thought of doing that to another man never even crossed my mind. But, the image of having you all kinked out in front of me does things to my head and body that are likely illegal."

"Feelings and thoughts are mutual," Cody murmured and pulled me in for a kiss. "I have no clue what it is about you that makes me want to be tied up, gagged, and whipped, but it's a fantasy that took root and hasn't stopped growing."

"Then let's make it happen. Okay? Soon?"

"I'm down," Cody agreed.

"Can I fuck you before we do any leather play?" I asked shyly. "It's been a long time since I took a man. I'd likely bust a nut within seconds if I tried to fuck you in leather the first time."

"You can fuck me anytime, anywhere, with or without leather." Cody kissed me again. "Maybe we should get out of here before we forget we weren't going to get indecent for the cameras and future children?"

"Yeah, probably a good idea." I laughed and we used our hands to paddle our tube to the next ladder.

Cody pulled the ring from the river and returned it to its proper place before following me to the locker room.

I turned and pounced on him as soon as we were inside the locker room. Pressing him up against the wall in a darkened corner, I shoved my knee between his legs and thrust my still hard cock against his hip as I devoured his mouth. "Never thought I'd say this, but maybe we should offer Jay a thank you."

Cody laughed into my kiss. "Maybe. But, let's enjoy making him think we're going to kill him for a little longer."

I ran my hands down Cody's back and took his ass in my hands. "This is mine. Next time we're together, if the timing and place is right, I want to own this beautiful ass."

"Beautiful, huh?"

"Stop, you know you've got the perfect bubble butt. Honestly, such a waste on a top." I delved my hands down the waist of his shorts until I could trace a finger along his crack. His shiver heated my blood, and I felt my dick leak against my own trunks.

"Never had reason or want to offer my *bubble butt* to someone." Cody rolled his eyes as he threw his head back against the wall as I skimmed my finger against his hole. "Maybe I was just waiting for the right guy to give it to."

I kissed him again then. Hard and punishing as my finger dipped into his tight hole. "Have you ever been fucked?" My knees almost gave out when he shook his head.

"I've had toys and fingers, but never a real cock." Cody rocked his hips against mine.

"Fuck, it's like I've died and gone to heaven." I drew in a ragged breath and rested my forehead against Cody's chest. "So, we'll be a plethora of firsts."

"No one I'd rather share those firsts with."

"So, are we like the common *enemies to lovers* trope in romance novels?" I pulled back and took a deep breath knowing we needed to get dressed and get out of there.

"Romance novels?" Cody cocked a brow. "Um, I wouldn't know. I don't read romance novels. Do you?"

I blushed. "Maybe. My mom read them. But, all I could ever find in them was het sex. I used to read them just to read about the guy. But, a few years ago, I realized there are gay romance novels. They aren't *all* my cup of tea, and honestly, I think a lot are written mostly for middle-aged straight women, but the sex is hot as fuck and I fall a little bit in love with the characters in almost every book I read." I lifted my chin defiantly. Would Cody laugh? Call me a pansy?

"You have any I can borrow?" Cody shoved from the wall and headed toward where we'd hung our clothes. "Sounds interesting. I've never been much of a reader, too busy with work, but I'd give it a try if you say it's good."

I smiled. "Yeah, you can borrow some."

"Enemies to lovers, huh?" Cody smirked. "Yeah, I guess that's what we'd be considered."

We dressed and headed back to Blueridge Junction. It was about eleven when we reached town.

"Can you swing by the B & B? I just want to check things out and make sure Dad is doing okay."

"Sure thing." I turned left toward the center of town instead of heading up Blueridge Hill.

We pulled up in front of the restaurant only to find Vicki Stringer blocking the door and holding up what looked to be picket-like signs.

"What the ever-loving fuck is this?" Cody grumbled.

"Hey, let's watch for just a second." I put my hand on his leg. "Call your dad and see if he knows she's out here."

Cody called his dad, asked about Stringer, laughed, and hung up. "Yeah, he knows. He's been letting people in through the side door when they can't get past her. She's been here about thirty minutes."

At that moment, Stringer's son, Matt showed up. Cody and I climbed from the car and walked to the sidewalk to see how the scene was going to play out.

Matt and another guy, presumably a date, walked toward the front door. It was easy to see when Matt recognized his mother. Shoulders slumped, glancing around, Matt approached his mom as Cody and I moved closer.

Matt grabbed the elbow of the guy he was with and said something in his ear and watched until the other guy walked around Vicki and entered the building.

"Mom, what the heck are you doing?" Matt ran a hand through his hair.

"Matty, I'm saving you from yourself and this terrible place." Vicki reached out to stroke Matt's face but he backed away.

"Mom, this has got to stop. You never should have come here." Matt took a deep breath and tried to walk around his mother.

"Matt, this isn't you. This isn't the town for you. This place isn't *you*. It's trashy and dirty and just plain wrong. I didn't raise you this way. My baby boy was taught to have morals." Vicki's words grew more and more pleading.

Matt clenched his jaw. "Mom, I'm not having this discussion again. I moved to BJ for work. I like it here. The B & B is a restaurant. End of story."

"Don't call it that disgusting name. *Blueridge Junction* may have been a quaint little Midwestern town at some point in the past, but the filth taking over is running it into the ground. I know what happens at this sanctuary of sin on Sundays. Perversion, sodomy, and the spread of disease both physical and spiritual. I can't have you here. I'll lose you to the devil and never get you back." Vicki dropped her picket sign and wrung her hands as her voice got more high pitched.

"Mom. I'm gay. Period. The only way you'll lose me is if you refuse to accept me for who I am. Now, I'm not going to leave my date waiting. I'm starving, and he's a lot better company than you right now." Matt reached out and touched Vicki's shoulder. "I'd love to have a relationship with you, but you've got to get yourself under control before that can happen. I won't submit myself to this ranting and raving." Matt stepped around his mom and walked into the B & B leaving Vicki with her mouth gaped open.

"You'll regret this, Matty! This whole place is going to be struck by the mighty hand of God. You'll be struck down with all the other sinners, left to burn for eternity in Hell, unless you repent. I'll pray with you, son. Leave this wicked place." Vicki's words clawed their way from a voice growing more and more hoarse.

"Ma'am, I'm going to have to ask you to remove yourself from the premises." I stepped forward and spoke to Ms. Stringer.

"It's a free country, and I have freedom of speech. I'm not hurting anyone. The likes of *these* types of people don't deserve protecting." Vicki continued with her rant.

"Ma'am, unless I'm mistaken, you have no permit to picket on this property." I stood my ground, silently preparing for her to bolt or knee my nuts.

"Fine, I'll go in the middle of the street." Vicki grabbed her signs and started pacing in the middle of the road.

"Ms. Stringer, I'll have to ask you to remove yourself from the street. Blueridge Junction doesn't allow picketing or protesting without a permit."

When Vicki started to argue, I continued. "And, you'll find yourself hard pressed to be issued a permit if your picketing involves threats, hate speech, and blatant bigotry. Not to mention, the B & B could press charges against you right now for disorderly conduct and disrupting their business. Even your son could press charges for the threats you made against him."

"I did no such thing!" Vicki shrieked.

"Ms. Stringer, I'll ask you again to leave the premises before I call for an on-duty officer to come arrest you." I kept my cool, something I was known for doing, but I feared Vicki was just unbalanced enough to cause a problem at any second.

"Mark my words," Vicki growled. "This place, this town, and these people are nothing but evil. Born of evil, practicing evil, and they'll die evil unless they turn from their wicked, sinful ways." She gathered her signs and stalked off to her car.

"That was pretty fucking amazing," Cody spoke at my side.

"Eh, standard protocol with a disorderly." Knowing Cody was impressed warmed something deep inside.

"Seriously though, you were so calm, cool, and collected. And sounded like a total badass telling her what to do and what was going to happen to her." Cody nuzzled against my ear. "I'm so turned on with your hot officer persona right now."

I laughed. "I may have taken a few liberties with some of what I said. I doubt any charges pressed against her would stick, at least not for what she was doing tonight. And, if she worked it right, she could likely get a permit to picket."

"I don't care. That was hot as fuck." Cody kissed at my ear and growled. "Just added something to my bucket list."

I shivered. "Yeah, what's that?"

"You, cop uniform, handcuffs, restraints, going all officer of the law on my ass. Literally and figuratively. I want to hear you read me the proverbial riot act." Cody groaned.

"That can definitely be arranged." I grabbed his ass. "I'm sure there are all sorts of things you've done wrong. Tell me, have you broken laws? Been a bad, bad boy?" I bit my lip and imagined stripping Cody bare and having my way with him. "Do you need this pretty ass spanked to help teach you a lesson?"

"Fuuuck," Cody moaned. "We need to stop or head directly to your place."

I smacked his ass. "Nah, it's late. I've got shifts coming up and you've got to work tomorrow, right? We aren't going to rush things. We've got time."

Cody reached to adjust himself as I did the same, and we headed into the B & B to check on things before I took him home.

CHAPTER 13

CODY

As we pulled up the drive, I knew I wasn't ready for the night to end.

"You want to hang out? Maybe go for a walk?" I hoped I didn't sound as desperate as I felt.

"It's getting late, and it's pretty chilly," Kennedy hedged.

"If you've got places to be, no biggie. But, if you're just cold, I'll keep you warm." I winked even as the cliché spilled from my mouth.

Kennedy laughed. "I can hang for a while."

We bypassed my parents' house. I knew Mom would be reading or crocheting in her favorite chair while waiting on Dad to get home. I saw Sadie's light in the basement, and her car was in the drive, so she was home safe. Arriving at the door to my place, saying guest house seemed weird, I gestured toward the front door. "Come in? Or take a walk?"

"Walk. I haven't been up on Blueridge very much." Kennedy glanced around at the land bathed in brilliant moonlight. "I've been up here, but never out on the land. Give me the tour."

I smiled and held out my hand. A couple months ago, I would have laughed in someone's face if they'd told me I'd voluntarily entertain Kennedy Marks on my family's property, holding his hand, and trying to figure out a way to prolong what had been the best date in my entire life.

Kennedy raised a brow and smirked as he reached for my hand. "Is this as surreal to you as it is to me?"

"The way the moonlight makes everything seem other worldly?" I bit my lip trying not to laugh. "Yeah, it's crazy. But, that's one of the beautiful things about living on Blueridge Hill. It's like we're closer to the moon, closer to the stars, and closer to the magic."

Kennedy gave me a look. "Mmhm, it's gorgeous up here, but that's not what I meant and you know it."

I laughed. "Yeah, I know. And, yes, this whole evening has been surreal. I just don't get it. How could we have hated each other so much, from the first time we even knew of the other's existence, and yet now we're on a date, holding hands, walking the woods, and hopefully ending the evening with goodnight kisses?"

"It's like that old saying, 'A fine line between love and hate.'" Kennedy mused for a moment before jerking his head toward me. "Not that I *love* you, but…," he stammered.

We reached an ancient oak tree, and I pulled Kennedy with me as I leaned my back against the massive trunk. "I get what you're saying. I never really understood that saying. I'm not saying I *love* you either." I dropped my chin but brought my gaze up to meet Kennedy's intense stare. "Yet." I frowned. "But I could. Damn it. I've never even contemplated this with anyone else, but I totally could see myself falling hard for you."

Kennedy was quiet for a moment. "Why?"

"Why what?"

"Why could you fall for me? I'm nothing. If it's just the whole top/bottom thing or the fact you feel comfortable telling me you want to be the sub to my dom. I don't know if that's enough to base love on." Kennedy wrinkled his brow.

"Stop." I jerked him closer, my hands tightening around his hips. "You are so much more than nothing. You are an amazing police officer, a son your parents are proud of, a great friend, and you spar with me better than anyone ever." I cupped his cheek. "Yes, the whole top/bottom, dom/sub, leather play thing has me tied in knots and anxiously awaiting the next step. But even without that, once I was able to see past the hatred, I recognized you as someone I absolutely enjoy spending time with."

Kennedy cocked his head and watched me.

"I've never been at a loss for hookups and one-night-stands and casual sex. But, a real connection grown from an actual relationship, be that friendship or enemies, is something I've never had." I traced my thumb over Kennedy's lips. "Never thought I'd want it. Definitely wasn't looking for it." I pulled his mouth closer and whispered, "But, I think I'm damn glad to have the chance to see what we can make of it."

Kennedy closed his eyes as my mouth took his.

I wrapped my arms around him to absorb his shiver and groan as my tongue dipped deep to tease his. Seconds, minutes, time was lost to us, but we finally broke and, breathing heavily, rested our foreheads together.

"I have never made out just for the sake of making out," Kennedy whispered. "It's always been the beginning of something more. And it never felt as real as that just did."

"Same here."

"Why does this feel so much different?" Kennedy asked the question my head and heart were posing as well.

"Maybe because it *is* different. Neither of us have done a real relationship, so this is all new and different. Maybe we see it as more important? More to lose? More to gain?" I shrugged.

"Yeah, I can see that." Kennedy nodded. "I've never went into any hook up or play scene or casual sex with the thought of it turning into something more."

"If you're like me, you've also barely known the person or people. Or you've known them on an intimate level or as an acquaintance and known nothing would ever grow from it." I thought back to all the guys I'd been with. None had ever worked their way into my heart and my life the way Kennedy had.

"Definitely." Kennedy smiled softly, his face aglow in the moonlight. "I guess we shouldn't question it, just enjoy?"

"I'm game if you are."

Kennedy nodded. "Come on, you haven't shown me much of the hill."

We walked for about thirty minutes while I pointed out places Levi, Micah, and I had played as children. I also showed him the drive that led to Micah and Cole's new house, and the permanently worn paths the guys and I would walk to each other's houses on a daily basis up through high school and beyond.

"You and Levi and Micah have always been close, huh?" Kennedy asked.

"Like brothers." I agreed. "Levi and Micah are cousins, but we've always been thick as thieves whether blood related or not."

"Ever have anything for either of them?"

I laughed. "Micah and I *may* have been caught in a compromising position by Levi. And, once Levi knew we were both of the same mind as he was, Levi and I *maybe* played around a bit. But, neither of them were more than just some hormonal teens figuring out their sexuality and finding out what felt good." I smiled at the memories. "I love them both and would die for them. The fooling around was great at the time because we had nothing to compare it to. But, nah, I can't see me working out in a relationship with either of them. Even before Cole and Jay came into the picture."

"They seem to really love each other." Kennedy mused.

"Micah and Cole? Definitely, such a perfect match. Makes a person believe in the saying, there's someone out there for everyone." I maneuvered us back toward the house. "And Levi and Jay are the absolute poster children for opposites attract and daddy/son if you want to get kinky with it." Once we reached the house, I faced Kennedy. "You want to come in?"

He mulled over my question. "Very much so," he began. "But, I'm going to say no."

I frowned and felt my heart burst just a little. "Why?"

"I've got a string of shifts starting tomorrow. You've got work. If I come in, we aren't going to sleep any time soon and it's already after midnight." Kennedy stepped in and whirled me around to press my back against the porch column. Grasping my head in both his hands, he devoured my mouth. His icy lips and chin and nose, bumping mine. "But, we definitely need to make plans for our next date and whatever else may come with that."

I nodded, nipping at his lips, unwilling to let him go. "I'm all for that. Are you going to be able to help with the rock wall at the Blue Jay?"

"Yeah, I'll be there. Sounds fun." Kennedy backed away and headed toward his car. "Jay said we can all try it out. Of course, that's more for him to find out if anyone is going to fall and break something than being nice, but I'm going to take full advantage." Kennedy waved. "I'll call or text."

I waved back, watched his car back up, and turn around before heading down the hill. Staring after him until his brake lights were no more, I took a deep breath. Pausing for a moment before going inside, I let my mind calm. Had I ever felt so content? *No.* Whatever this thing with Kennedy had turned into was a like a gigantic gift waiting to be opened. I wanted to tear into it, but I also wanted to savor these feelings and take my time. I smiled into the moonlit night and took my quivering ball of thoughts and plans and emotions inside for a shower and bed.

"Thank you for your help," Jay said to the three local guys who had installed the rock wall. "We'll get all the rocks tightened and test it out."

I was glad the professionals had been there because putting up that rock wall was no job for amateurs.

"Don't hesitate to call us if it seems like something isn't right." David shook Jay's hand as the men left.

Jay turned to all of us and rubbed his hands together. "Are my boys ready?"

"You seem extremely excited about this." Cole chuckled.

Jay blushed. "I just can't believe we were able to get this rock wall donated and installed. I mean, I had hoped for one about a year down the road, but having it for the opening means a lot."

Levi pulled Jay close to his side and kissed his head. "People believe in what you're doing here, babe. It's a good thing. A lot of the community and even those outside of BJ want to see the Blue Jay succeed."

"And a lot of that is because of all of you." Jay looked at all of us with tears in his eyes. "Seriously, thank you for all you've done to get the word out and the donations coming in. It's so amazing to see the money and items and services come rolling in."

"Just glad we can help." Cole smiled. "It's been really cool seeing how pumped people are to see the BJ get set up. So many of the staff in the school district are more than willing to offer tutoring. And a ton of the senior class students are on board with serving volunteer hours."

"Keep in mind that not *all* of Blueridge is on board with getting the Blue Jay up and running." Kennedy piped up. "Not trying to rain on the parade, but have to keep it real."

I nodded. "Yeah, Vicki Stringer is hell bent on shutting down Leather Sundays. Shit, she even wants the B & B closed. I'm one hundred percent certain she will cause similar issues with the Blue Jay."

"All she has to do is gather a few of the homophobic townsfolk." Kennedy agreed.

"I think she can gather a few of the opposition, but she's not been in town long enough to have gained respect or trust from most people." Levi shook his head. "Even those who aren't completely on board with the BJ are more likely to listen to townspeople who they know, trust, and respect than some lady who just moved here and is creating all sorts of chaos."

"Good thing dear ol' Dad is dead." Micah chuckled humorlessly. "Stringer would have had no problem recruiting *him* to her side. Or him recruiting her to his side."

"It's good to be prepared and know we'll face some opposition." Jay nodded. "But, for now, I say we get this rock wall finished and try this sucker out!"

"Do you have ladders?" I asked as I eyed the rocks higher up the wall.

"I think the guys took them with them." Jay frowned and bit his lip. "Clearly I need to get one to have here full time."

"No worries. We can handle it." Levi hunkered down and gestured to Jay to climb on his shoulders.

Jay threw his head back and cackled. "I love your mind, Daddy."

Levi threw a scathing look over his shoulder. "Just get your ass over here."

Levi stood with Jay on his shoulders then turned to me. "Hand him the screwdriver."

I dug around in the tools, found the screwdriver, and then handed it to Jay.

"Don't just stand there. Climb on, boys." Jay laughed and whooped and pretended the tool was a lasso as he whipped it around his head.

Micah grabbed a screwdriver and handed it to Cole before kneeling down to let Cole climb on.

"We'll just take care of the lower ones," I said.

"No way. This is too much fun. Pony up!" Jay squawked.

I glanced at Kennedy. "You wanna ride?"

Kennedy smirked and moved closer to me. "Anything to get your head between my legs, huh?"

"Well, if that's the way we're looking at it, maybe *I* should climb on so *your* head is between *my* legs." I winked.

"Or, I could get a bit and harness and ride you good." Kennedy teased.

"Jesus, you two! Get a damn room." Levi groused as he maneuvered Jay to tighten another rock.

"Or, maybe another basement." Cole laughed as Micah swayed him back and forth.

About ten minutes later, we had all the rocks tightened and secured.

"Time to take this baby for a spin!" Jay crowed as he clamored down from Levi's shoulders. "Harness up, boys!"

Cole, Jay, and I all grabbed harnesses and let the other guys strap us in and hook us up.

"Not *exactly* the harness I want to get you into, but this will do for now." Kennedy growled in my ear as he cinched the straps.

We spent the rest of the evening taking turns climbing, racing, and just having fun.

By the time we removed the harnesses, hung them up, and gathered our things, I noticed the weather had started to change.

"Dang, I knew it was supposed to start snowing, but this looks more like ice." Levi held out his hand to catch the falling precipitation. "Better get home before it gets bad."

"BJ's road crews will clear the streets as quickly as possible, but they can't clear it if it's coming down hard and fast." I zipped up my coat against the cold.

"The department works with the independent citizens who have plows on their trucks." Kennedy agreed. "But, clearing the streets with ice coming down is pointless. And dangerous. We don't want the contractors out in the ice. Best to just stay home if possible." He turned to me. "Can you close the restaurant if it gets bad?"

I lifted a shoulder. "We have before. But, it has to get really bad. If businesses are open in town, it's good for us to be open for employees to come in for meals."

"Micah, you close the auto shop?" Kennedy asked.

"I can, if it's super bad." Micah gestured toward the sky. "But, I'll wait to see if it gets worse before making that decision."

"Woohoo, I bet we get a snow day!" Cole boasted and received only groans from the rest of us.

"I don't have any appointments lined up," Levi added. "If it gets too bad, I'll keep the shop closed."

"Mmmm, we can stay in bed and cuddle all day." Jay snuggled up against Levi's chest.

"Okay, well, if it gets super bad, I want you all to stay home," Kennedy warned. "Ice isn't something to play around with. Most this town has four-wheel drive, but that's useless against ice."

We all said our goodbyes and headed toward our vehicles.

I pulled Kennedy into my arms, nuzzled his neck, and laughed when he jerked away, complaining of my cold nose. "What about you?" I asked.

"What about me?" Kennedy frowned.

"Can you call off work? Will the department change shifts because of the weather?"

Kennedy smirked. "Police officers don't get the luxury of calling off. In fact, I'll be busier during an ice storm than any regular shift. They'll likely call in extras and have us working longer."

I cupped his cheek with my gloved hand. "Promise me you'll be super careful? Stay in touch?"

Kennedy grabbed my head in both hands and kissed me deeply. "Promise. I have a lot to look forward to. Just the thought of our plans will keep me going through crazy icy shifts."

"Damn right you've got a lot to look forward to. Just like I do." I kissed him back. "Text me once you're home."

"Will do. Be careful going up the hill. Sleep tight and stay safe." Kennedy brushed one last kiss against my lips and climbed into his car.

I watched him drive away before climbing into my truck. I made my way home like I was on a gigantic slip-n-slide. Saying a silent prayer once I parked my truck at home, I texted all the BJ Boys to be sure they had made it home safely.

Knowing all my guys were home safe and sound, I checked in on Sadie.

"Shouldn't you be heading to bed?" I asked as I headed down the stairs to her basement room.

"Fingers crossed for a snow day." Sadie grinned as she broke her gaze from her phone.

"Fair enough," I chuckled. "If there's no snow day, let me know and I'll drive you to school. It's getting bad out there." I leaned down to kiss her head before heading upstairs to say goodnight to my parents.

"What do you think about opening tomorrow?" Dad paused the television show he was watching. "Your mom prefers we not travel in this ice."

"It's bad out there. No one needs to be traveling in it," Mom protested.

"Let's wait to see what it's like in the morning. Maybe we'll open late? If the businesses around town are open then I think we should be, too." I leaned down to kiss my mom's head and chucked my dad on the shoulder. "I'll check in with you in the morning."

After almost breaking my neck walking to the guesthouse, I showered, climbed into bed, and spent the next hour "sexting" with Kennedy before drifting to sleep.

Chapter 14

Kennedy

"Sure thing, Captain." I nodded at my boss the next morning when I got to work. "Just let me tell a couple people where I'm going." I shook my cell phone.

"Think it's wise to do that, son?" Captain frowned. "May just end up worrying loved ones needlessly."

I thought about his words. *Loved ones* echoed through my head. My parents fit that description. Did Cody fall in that category? "Nah, my mom and friends would kick my ass if they found out I was out in this weather on a call-out and didn't let them know."

Captain chuckled. "Well, you know them better than I do. Take care of what you need to." He pointed toward the front of the station. "We'll meet up front. Be sure to wear your weather gear. It's a cold ass bitch out there. Boots will be the best way to keep yourself upright instead of flat on your ass."

I laughed before thumbing my phone screen to open the texts.

The first text went to my mom and dad.

Gotta go help with traffic over in Ashville. Don't stress. Will text when I can.

A few seconds later, Mom replied.

Okay. We'll keep the scanner on. Love you. Be safe.

Love you, too.

Then to Cody.

Hey, got called over to Ashville to help with traffic issues. The hills over there are more traveled than BJ, and they are having a lot of crashes and slide offs.

Moments later, Cody shot back a text.

That doesn't sound fun. Can I help in any way?

I smiled to myself. Just like Cody to offer help. Also just like Cody to want to be involved so he knew what was going on.

Nah, department called in extras. Not sure how long I'll be over there. May not be able to answer texts. Just didn't want you to think I'm ignoring you.

I watched the screen, hoping Cody would reply before I needed to head out. Finally, I slid my phone into my inner coat pocket and headed toward the front of the station. Pulling my boots on before grabbing my skullcap, I searched for gloves. My phone buzzed against my chest seconds before I put on my gloves.

Going to Levi's. Everyone going to hang out there. Come over when shift is done.

My heart swelled and I couldn't help the goofy smile that filled my face. The invite would give me something to look forward to while out in the ice and cold. But, it would also make me anxious to finish my shift and bust ass back to BJ. I thumbed a quick reply.

Will do. Keep a spot on the couch warm for me.

Somehow, knowing Cody and the guys were all together and waiting for me to get back home to BJ put a little skip in my step and made the next twelve hours seem not so daunting.

I spoke too soon thinking the shift would be easier knowing Cody was waiting on me. Icy roads were a complete and total bitch. Snowplows were useless. After two of Ashville's trucks slid off the road, their police department demanded the plows stay off the roads.

"Gonna have to wait until the ice melts. Wrecking the plows isn't helping anyone." Ashville's police captain spoke over his steaming mug of coffee as we all took a quick break to warm up before heading back out. "The mayor has officially closed the city down. So, the only traffic we have to deal with are people trying to get back home after the declaration was made and those who are still stuck in wrecks or slide offs."

I spent the next twelve hours rotating between manning the phones at the Ashville station, walking to and from accidents to help victims get back into town, and assisting the paramedics triage the injured. Thankfully, most of the wrecks were not serious and many of the townspeople were grateful for help in getting back to their homes.

By the time the twelve hours were done, we had frozen toes, frozen fingers, and frozen noses. But all the people stuck in the ice had been rescued and the few injuries had been treated or were safe in the Ashville hospital. Thank God there had been enough officers to rotate so everyone could all rest for an hour or so between being out in the cold.

"Can't say thank you enough to the Blueridge department for helping out their neighboring town in a time of need." Ashville's captain gave us all a firm handshake. "Now, get on out of here."

"Okay, men, looks like we can take our leave. Ashville is closed until the ice melts. Let's get our sorry asses back to BJ. I don't know about you, but I plan to use up all the hot water, drink a gallon of coffee, and spend the rest of the night warming up." Our captain herded us out of the Ashville station. "Don't worry about going by the station. I'll take care of any paperwork. The new shift will be showing up about the time we roll into town." Captain gave us all a stern look. "But, boys, if I don't hear from each and every one of you within an hour, I'll personally search you out and kick your ass. Check in. You hear?"

I nodded wearily and climbed into my vehicle to begin the treacherous journey back to BJ. Thankfully, the state trucks had been out with salt brine to help with the highway between Ashville and Blueridge so the trip home wasn't terrible until I reached the hills of BJ.

When my car finally slid to a stop at the four-way stop, I seriously considered my options. A left turn would take me to my place where I could eat, shower, and sleep. Alone. A straight shot through town and up the hill would take me to Levi's. Where I'd find my friends—and Cody. I knew food would be plentiful. I could shower. And I could sleep.

And...Cody.

With very little contemplation, I drove through BJ and headed up the hill. Twenty minutes later, I resigned myself to the fact that my car wasn't making it up Blueridge Hill. I glanced down at my heavy coat, top of the line winter boots, and my warm gloves. Quickly, I parked my car at the base of the hill and began the hellish and icy hike up to Levi's house.

The thought of Cody waiting on me in a warm, loving, safe home at the top of the hill was the only thing that kept me climbing.

By the time I reached Levi's, I couldn't feel my toes, my lips, or my nose. I was pretty sure snot was frozen to my face, and I probably had icicles on my eyebrows. But, I stomped up the steps and banged on the door with a pounding in my heart and a smile on my frozen face.

Cody yanking the door open and pulling me into his arms was probably one of the top ten best moments in my life.

~~*

"Thank the good Lord above." Jay hollered from the kitchen. "We were about ready to put him out in the cold if he didn't stop worrying himself sick about his leather daddy."

Cody's arms tightened around me as he maneuvered us around a corner away from the guys. Kissing me deeply, his hands trapping my face and tipping my head so he could thoroughly ravish my mouth, Cody finally broke the kiss and rested his head against mine.

"Hi," I whispered.

"Hi," he whispered back. "So, yeah, I may have been a bit concerned about you being out in the weather."

"Awww, that's sweet. I'm not sure anyone has ever worried about me except my mom and dad." I peppered kisses over his face.

Levi popped his head around the corner. "Food? Drink? Shower?"

"Yes," I sighed. "All of the above."

Levi laughed. "We'll work on the food and drink if you want to work on the shower." Levi glanced between the two of us, waggling his brow.

"The basement bathroom would be the most private and keep you from hogging the restroom up here for people who need to use it." Cody nodded with a serious look on his face as if he was truly just concerned about the convenience of others.

Levi simply laughed and walked away.

I narrowed my eyes and turned Cody to back him against the wall. "I think we need a revisit of the infamous basement."

"Nah," Cody murmured. The heat of his blush warming my lips. "I wouldn't want to intrude."

Fisting the front of his shirt in my hand, I pressed him hard to the wall. "Wasn't asking. Not open for discussion."

Cody watched me for a split second before a wicked gleam overtook his face. "Maybe I don't feel like a shower. What are you going to do to make it worth my time?"

Keeping his shirt in one hand, I nudged at his left arm and gripped his right hand to lift it over his head. Once both arms were pinned against the wall,

I rotated my hips against his. "I think I owe you that ass spanking I promised a while ago. And once I get that beautiful ass good and dirty, I'll be sure to clean it, stroke it, kiss it, and pamper it until you can't remember your damn name."

Cody's eyes filled with what looked like a fiery challenge. He bit his lip, shrugged a shoulder, and replied with a bored, "Eh" punctuated with a single thrust of his hips.

"Get your ass down to the basement and strip." I nipped at his jawline and growled into his ear. "I've been running on pure adrenaline for the past twelve hours. Your smart mouth and cocky challenges will get you exactly the punishment you're wanting."

"Who says I'm wanting?" Cody jutted his chin.

Releasing his shirt, I cupped his dick in my palm. "No one has to say anything. This beautiful boy is speaking loud and clear." I nuzzled his ear. "Now, be a good boy and follow my directions. Testing me will only earn you harder punishment."

Cody's air of confident behavior flickered for a split second, but I saw the longing in his eyes. "Promise?" he whispered.

"Get your ass down there, naked, and waiting for me and find out if I keep my promises." I shoved him toward the basement door and smacked his ass as he walked away.

Before I headed to the basement to shower, I popped my head into the living room where the crew was playing Cards Against Humanity. "We'll be up later." I winked and all of them laughed.

"We'll be here." Micah chuckled.

"I think they are officially together in case anyone was wondering," Cole joked and the rest of the group laughed, but I was already gunning toward the basement.

By the time I reached the bathroom, Cody was stark naked and had the shower started. He turned as I walked into the tiny space. I peeled the remainder of my uniform from my body.

"Let's see what you've got, Officer."

I reached around him to turn off the water. "Don't want to waste water." I shoved him toward the bed in the main part of the basement. "On your knees, ass up."

Cody turned on me and came chest to chest. "Make me," he challenged.

"Why you gotta fight? You and I both know you're craving my hand marking your ass just as much as I am." I spun him around, held his hands tight behind his back, and nudged him forward with my knee. "Now, get on your knees and show me that pretty ass."

The shiver that traveled through Cody's body echoed the anticipation in me. When my man crawled onto the bed and raised his ass, opening himself to me, I nearly lost it. I cupped the round globes of flesh and squeezed. "So damn gorgeous." Moving to Cody's side, I smacked his ass. Hard. I'd never in my life seen anything sexier than the way his skin pinked. Cody's moan indicated he enjoyed the spanking. "You want more?"

Cody nodded.

"Say it," I demanded.

"I want more," Cody gasped.

"Want what? Say it."

"Spank me."

"Say my name."

"Spank me, Kennedy," Cody begged.

Over the next few moments, my hand made solid contact with Cody's increasingly hot and red ass.

Cody cursed, squirmed, and panted under me.

Between smacks, my lips and tongue followed the caresses of my hands like a soothing balm. When Cody reached for his dick, I spanked his ass harder and knocked away his hand. "Uh-uh, that's mine. I'll take care of that." Stroking Cody's cock, spanking his ass, and leaning in to growl in his ear, I brought him to the brink of release time and time again until his knees gave out and he collapsed to the bed with a strangled cry.

"God, please baby. Let me come." Cody thrust his hips against the bed.

"I want everyone to know this cock is *mine*. One day, I want it in a cage, only accessible to me, so I know I *own* your pain and your pleasure." I pulled his back to my chest and reached around to stroke his throbbing dick. Teasing at his ear with my lips, pinching and twisting his nipple, and rocking my leaking cock against his ass, I jacked him until he lost control and came in long creamy ropes on his stomach.

When Cody shuddered the last of his release, I cupped his balls and commanded in his ear, "Get yourself into the shower. I'm going to fuck that beautiful mouth and come down your throat."

Cody whimpered.

"You hear me?"

Cody nodded.

"Then get ready for a mouth fucking like you've never had, baby." I pushed him off the bed and followed him to the bathroom where he immediately started the shower and climbed in. "On your knees," I demanded.

My heart soared when Cody dropped to his knees without a single bit of hesitation. I lost myself completely when he gripped my hips and nuzzled his nose into the base of my dick.

Cody's gaze lifted to meet mine at the exact moment his lips opened and engulfed my pulsing length into his wet and warm mouth.

Cody sucked me up and down a few times before relaxing his mouth and challenging me with his eyes.

"You got something to say?" I growled.

Popping off my cock for only a second, Cody mouthed off. "I believe you promised me the best mouth fuck I've ever had. Just waiting to get it started."

Gripping his hair in one hand and my dick in the other, I slapped his lips with my hard length. "Open up."

Cody smirked, tongued the bead of come from my head, and sucked me deep. His hands on my hips pulled me closer, swallowing me down, begging me to increase the speed and power. What my bad boy wanted, he'd get. I let loose and allowed my cock to piston deep and hard, my head pounding the back of his throat.

Cody brought a hand to cup my balls, fondled, twisted, and fingered my ass. The moment his wet finger breached my ass, my balls drew up tight, and I shot my load hard and fast, coating the back of his throat. Feeling as if my lungs and heart were going to explode from the exertion and the overwhelming emotions, I took in the muscle man on his knees in front of me, sucking my cock dry, a happy dazed look on his face.

"Fuuuuck." I shuddered as Cody licked the last of my come from his lips and pulled himself to stand. "That was amazing."

"So damn amazing," Cody agreed and wrapped me in his arms as the hot water poured down.

"But, I gotta wash before I collapse." I laughed, completely exhausted. "And I need food. Stat."

Cody washed himself quickly before turning to run soapy hands through my hair. I clutched his ass when the soapy touch caressed my dick, balls, and ass.

"Ouch," Cody hissed.

"What's wrong?" I pulled back.

"My ass stings like a mother fucker."

I smiled, my heart filling and my dick making a valiant effort to swell to life again. "Mmmm, I love knowing you'll feel me there every time you sit down tonight."

"I love knowing your hand print is marked in red all over my ass," Cody murmured against my ear.

When the water began to run cold, we climbed from the shower and toweled off. Cody wrapped a towel around his waist and bounded up the stairs returning a few moments later with soft, warm clothes for us to wear.

He found me sprawled on the bed, quickly losing the battle to keep my eyes open.

"Come on. Baby. There's food upstairs." He pulled me from the bed and planted a kiss on me. "You can sleep, but you need food and drink first."

We emerged from the basement to find knowing grins and wagging brows. But salad, pizza, breadsticks, milk, and water greeted me too. My stomach growled loudly, and I didn't even care that every single one of the BJ Boys knew what had just went down. My only priority was food and sleep.

CHAPTER 15

CODY

"Shhh," I hissed once again.

"Dude, he's sleeping like the dead. He's not moved a single inch." Micah chuckled.

"Still, we don't have to be so loud. Let him sleep." Was this how a new parent felt with a sleeping baby in the house?

Kennedy stretched on my lap. "S'okay, I'm awake."

Jay and Cole winced. "Sorry," they both whispered as I glared at them.

"Nah, I was waking for a while. Thanks for letting me sleep." Kennedy sat up on the couch and rubbed his eyes before running both hands through his mussed hair. "Damn, how long was I out?"

"Couple hours." I massaged his shoulder. "You want to go to bed so you can sleep better?"

"Nope, the nap was enough. I'll sleep more later to get ready for tomorrow's shift." Kennedy took the bottle of water I handed him.

"You seriously have to go back tomorrow?" I groused. "You'd think they'd give you some time off after the hell you just went through."

Kennedy smiled. "That would be nice, but every officer was either on-shift or called in. If we all got tomorrow off, who would do the work?" He drained the water. "It's cool. I'll sleep later tonight and be good as new for tomorrow." Kennedy's stomach grumbled. "Damn, I know we ate before I crashed, but is there more food? I'm fuckin' starving."

"Yep," Levi stood from his place beside Jay on the couch. "Come on."

"Dude, you don't have to fix it for me." Kennedy blushed but followed Levi to the kitchen.

"Nah, I could eat." Levi rubbed his stomach. "Gotta keep the Daddy physique for my greedy bottom boy over there." He glanced over toward Jay and winked.

Jay laughed and kissed the air. "You know I love that Daddy bod," Jay crowed.

Kennedy and Levi disappeared into the kitchen. Soon, sounds of food being prepped filled the air.

"So, are you guys just playing?" Jay raised a brow in question.

"Huh?"

"Don't play dumb, Cody. It's not becoming." Jay pursed his lips. "Are you and Kennedy just scratching an itch? Playing? Sharing your kinks? Or is it real?"

I paused for a moment before answering Jay's question and allowed my thoughts to run freely through my head. "You know, before the basement prison, and even immediately after, I would have said we were just getting each other out of our systems."

Jay hung on my words, his eyes gleaming. "And now?"

Micah and Cole stopped whatever conversation they were having to hear my answer.

"Now? Now I'd say it's definitely not just play. I mean, we have our love of leather. Lots of plans for kink and play. But, even without any of that, I like being around him. And I'm pretty sure he feels the same." I smiled and felt my cheeks heat.

"Like love? A true relationship? Forever type stuff?" Jay bounced on the couch in his giddiness.

"I can't speak for him, and I'm not making predictions about the future, but for now I'd call it a relationship. And *love* is a bit scary, but extreme *like* is accurate. At least on my part." I glanced toward the kitchen, thinking about Kennedy.

"Well, from the way he looks at you, I'd say the feeling is mutual." Micah piped up.

"Agreed." Jay nodded.

"I haven't been around as long as the rest of the group," Cole began. "Why did you guys hate each other so much?"

I shook my head. "It's weird. I remember *hating* him. Like, I couldn't stand to be around him, speak to him, or even just look at him. But, as far as *why*, I can't explain it."

"Like I said, a very fine line exists between love and hate, and I think you and Kennedy have been teasing that line for a long time." Jay preened on the couch, puffed up like a damn peacock. "Personally, I think it was the basement idea that pushed you well on your way to crossing that line. And, you two took it from there and haven't looked back."

"Yeah, yeah," I huffed and rolled my eyes. "You're the hero."

"If the high heel fits, I'll wear that shoe like the damn diva bitch I am." Jay stood and sashayed around the living room like a model on the catwalk before blowing us a kiss and heading to the kitchen.

Micah, Cole, and I laughed and stood to join the other guys. While some ate, others played around on their phones, chitchat was comfortable, and the whole room filled with comfort and an overwhelming feeling of *rightness*.

"Dude," Cole directed his words to Jay. "Where were you when these before and after pics were taken?" He held up his phone for Jay to see.

"Oh," Jay smiled demurely, "those were a few weeks ago at a friend's bachelorette party. Levi and I went out with the girls for a while. Those pics are before the party and after."

Micah peeked at the pics on the phone screen. "Why are you in different clothes? Please tell me you didn't plan a wardrobe change."

"While a wardrobe change is sometimes the perfect way to turn a night around or change the mood, this wardrobe change was more of a necessity than a choice." Jay pursed his lips and batted his eyes.

We all stared at Jay, waiting on him to finish.

Levi chuckled. "Go ahead, baby, tell them why you had to change clothes."

"I puked all over the table in front of everyone. So I went to the bathroom to clean up." Jay blushed.

"That was before we got kicked out of the bar." Levi continued eating, simply smiling as his boy told the story.

"They kicked you out for puking? Harsh." Cole thumbed through more pics as he spoke.

"No. As I was going to clean myself up, I got stopped by security. He was like 'if you're puking it's time to go.' I don't fight security. I'm really reasonable when I'm drunk." Jay kept a straight face the whole time he was talking, and I realized he was being serious.

I couldn't help busting out laughing. "God, you are fuckin' one of a kind."

"It's true though, he's really incredibly reasonable when he's drunk." Levi gestured toward Jay with a fork as he spoke. "He's actually a lot more reasonable drunk than sober sometimes."

"Hey." Jay frowned and crossed his arms.

"Wouldn't have you any other way." Levi put his plate in the sink and gathered Jay in his arms, nuzzling the kid's neck and whispering something in his ear.

Jay threw his arms around Levi's neck. "Goodnight, boys. Feel free to stay as long as you'd like, but we have reservations for two in our bed." Jay wrapped his legs around Levi's waist and waved at us as they left the kitchen.

Micah and Cole took the foldout couch while Kennedy and I headed back to the basement. The rest of the night was quiet as the six of us slept, or didn't sleep as the case may have been, and by morning, I was glad to see the temperature had warmed enough to change the ice to rain. There were likely still slick spots, but the storm was over.

"Hey, can you drive me down to my car? I left it at the bottom of the hill." Kennedy asked as we dried off from a fairly tame shower.

"You *walked* up Blueridge in an ice storm?" My eyes nearly popped from my head.

"My car wouldn't do the ice on the incline." Kennedy shrugged.

"So you hiked up the hill? Why?"

"Wanted to see you." Kennedy blushed and bit his lip.

I cupped his face and kissed him, my tongue plunging deep. "I should kick your ass, but I'm also glad you braved the icy hill for me."

"Kick my ass?" Kennedy spun me around and shoved me against the wall. "I'd like to see you try." He bit at my bottom lip before tracing his tongue over the sting. "A guy will do crazy things when he's…" Kennedy's words trailed off.

Our eyes met, heat and desire flashed, and I longed to hear the rest of what he was going to say. Because I was beginning to think I felt exactly the same.

"…determined." Kennedy finished and dropped his gaze. "Gotta get to the station. Can you take me down the hill or should I ask one of the others?"

My heart twisted, turned, and fell. "No, I can take you. Let's go."

~~*

"Damn it," I bit out and tossed my phone on the bar's back counter at the B & B.

"Problem?" Dad asked.

I glanced at him and shrugged. "Kennedy."

"Trouble in paradise?" Dad stopped wiping down the glasses.

We were cleaning up at closing time.

"Not that I know of." I checked my phone screen again. "We had plans last night, but he got called in for an extra shift. He's not returned any of my calls or texts today."

"Maybe he's asleep."

"Yeah, probably." I knew my dad was likely right, but something wasn't sitting well with me. "Hey, you think you can finish up here?"

Dad cocked his head and smirked. "Going to check on him?"

"Yeah, just want to make sure he's okay." I grabbed my keys. "You got this?"

"Go on, get out of here." Dad shook his head as he chuckled and put the last glass away.

Kennedy's place was only a couple blocks from the B & B. I could have walked, but I didn't want to have to walk back after I found out Kennedy was just exhausted from his extra shift. Plus, I'd been at the restaurant since early morning, and I was feeling pretty damn wrung out myself.

The front of Kennedy's little garden apartment was dark, but light glowed in the back window. Crossing my fingers that he wouldn't mistake me for a burglar, I moved closer to the light and glanced in the window. Kennedy was sprawled at the kitchen table with enough beer bottles to restock the bar at the B & B.

"Shit," I hissed, immediately realizing *something* was wrong. My heart raced and my head spun trying to figure out just *what* was bothering him. Kennedy wasn't the type to go on a bender without a good reason.

I rounded the back of the apartment and knocked at the door. Kennedy's head lifted from the table, his glassy eyes struggling to focus before gesturing me in the door.

"Kennedy?" I hedged as I moved to where I could see his face plastered to the table.

"Heeeey, baaay-beeee," Kennedy slurred his words and gave me a drunken grin. "Come in. Join me. Have a drink."

"Babe, wanna tell me what's going on?" I quickly gathered all the empties and put the rest in the fridge. Better they were kept out of sight if I was going to get Kennedy sobered up.

"It's the anniversary," Kennedy mumbled against the table.

Anniversary? What the hell was he talking about? No way he was stumbling drunk over some lame-ass anniversary of us being together. Were we truly together? I thought we were, but we hadn't officially had the conversation.

"Anniversary?" I pulled him from the kitchen chair and walked him to the bathroom. "Here, sit on the stool for a bit. Gonna wash your face and get you some fresh clothes. You'll feel better."

"Clothes are fine," Kennedy argued.

"Baby, you stink like sweat and beer." I ran hot water on a washcloth before running the warm material over his face, behind his ears, and around his neck. I prayed he wouldn't puke, but it was a chance I had to take. "Hold the trashcan. Wait here." I rushed from the bathroom and got him a new shirt. Pants would wait until he wasn't so wobbly and woozy.

The sweaty shirt came off as easily as trying to dress dead weight—not easily at all. And getting Kennedy's head and arms through the new shirt was even more difficult. "Damn it. Stop squirming, and just let me put your arm where I need it."

Kennedy lifted his glazed eyes and then busted out laughing followed much too closely by a very wet hiccup. "And just where do you need my arm to be, baby? I didn't know you were into fisting." He fell against me in a fit of laughter.

"Come on, funny guy." I heaved him to his feet. Kennedy was shorter than me by an inch or so and not as bulky, but drunk-Kennedy was damn awkward to maneuver. "We're going to drink some water and then coffee. And you can tell me about whatever is bothering you."

I settled Kennedy on the couch with his trusty trashcan and handed him a bottle of water. "Don't move. Gonna start the coffee." I hurried to the kitchen to start the coffee pot. I had a feeling he and I were both going to need at least a few cups.

I returned to the living room and grabbed a blanket. Leaning against the arm of the couch, I pulled Kennedy's back to my chest and put the blanket over us.

"Wanna tell me about it?" I whispered in his ear.

"Twenty-two years…today," Kennedy mumbled and wiped at a tear.

"Take your time, babe. We've got all night." My heart clenched in anxiety and dread.

"He hated me. Beat the shit out of my mom mostly, but once I was mobile, he pretty much knocked me around daily. The older I got, I found it easier to take the punches, kicks, and slaps, but the words were the worst." Kennedy took a shuddery breath. "Mom tried to protect me, but she couldn't stop him when he really got going." His body shook against mine. "He made me sit on the couch, my nose throbbing and dripping blood, and one eye so swollen I couldn't even see from it. But, I could see…enough. He put her on her knees right in front of me, yanked her hair until she had no choice but to look straight at me. Tears streamed down her face. 'I'm sorry,' was all she had time to choke out before he blew her brains out and threw her to my feet."

Kennedy stopped, catching his breath on a sob before curling into me. "He pointed the gun at me. 'You're a worthless, weak piece of shit. Never been good at anything. No one has ever loved you. No one will ever love you. Not a damn person would miss you if I splattered your guts all over this house.' Then my Dad put the gun to the side of his head. 'But, I'll let you live just so you can die a thousand deaths every time you think about how hated you are, and how you couldn't save your own mother.' He pulled the trigger and fell in a heap on top of her."

Kennedy stopped talking, and I realized I'd been holding my breath.

Fuck.

Shit.

God *damn* it.

I gulped deep breaths and held him tightly, stroking his hair and whispering, "It's okay, baby. It's okay. He was wrong. So damn wrong. You are strong and important and loved. So fucking loved."

We sat like that until Kennedy chose to stirred.

"My legs are asleep. Gotta get up." He stretched before looking at me.

He wasn't completely sober, but he was no longer drunk.

"Thank you," Kennedy whispered. "Never told anyone all of that."

Tears welled in my eyes and stung my nose. "Thank you for trusting me. Every single part of that story made me sick and fucking pissed off, but thank you for giving me that part of yourself."

"You made coffee?" Kennedy asked.

"Yeah, maybe cold by now. But I can make more."

I stood and led him to the kitchen.

"Can I make a suggestion?" I held Kennedy in my arms as we lounged on his bed with the television playing softly. We'd had coffee, shared a sensual and revitalizing shower, and dozed in his bed for the past hour.

"Mmhm," Kennedy mumbled against my chest.

"Call off tomorrow." I braced myself for Kennedy's protest.

"Why? I'm not sick."

"You're emotionally and physically drained." I stroked a hand through his hair. "I think you could use a day off. Call it a mental health day."

Kennedy propped up on an elbow. "It feels weird to call off when I'm not sick. But, I'm not sure I'd be in the right headspace to be effective on shift."

I nodded.

"I'll do it." Kennedy's eyes gleamed, a mix of exhaustion, sadness, and challenge. "You spend the day with me?"

I started to protest. I was supposed to be at the B & B. But, the look Kennedy gave me hinted of hopefulness, and I couldn't say no. "You got it. We'll do a complete day of rest and relaxation. Recharge ourselves."

Kennedy reached for his phone and made the call as I grabbed my phone and walked from the room to call my dad to let him know I'd need to be off the next day.

"Kennedy okay?" Dad's concern was genuine. Leave it to my father not to question the insane time I was calling him or the fact I was leaving him on his own at the restaurant.

"Yeah. There was an issue, but not with us. He's fine physically. Just some emotional shit from the past wearing on him." My heart hurt and my fist clenched as I recalled the nightmare Kennedy had shared with me earlier. "Sorry to leave you in a lurch at the B & B."

"Don't sweat it. I'll call in a couple extras to help with the busy shifts. Your mom may even want to come help for a bit." Dad cleared his throat and the mattress creaked as he shifted in bed. "Just do what you need to do. Give Kennedy our best."

I returned to the bedroom to find Kennedy asleep, sprawled on the bed still holding his phone.

Slipping the phone from his hand before turning off the lamp, I pulled the covers down, crawled into bed and pulled Kennedy to my chest. He stirred and cuddled against me.

"Did you mean it?" Kennedy's question was muffled against my chest.

"Mean what?" I kissed the top of his head.

"That I'm loved?" His voice was small and quiet and so very unsure.

"I meant every damn word I said." I turned on the small lamp before tipping Kennedy's face up so he was looking at me. "You are *strong* and *important* and *loved.*"

"Never felt those things." Kennedy's eyes glistened.

"Well, they are true and don't you ever fuckin' forget it." I kissed him, soft and slow. "And even if *I* wasn't falling head over heels in love with you, you'd still have your parents, this town and the BJ

Boys who love you." The words weren't planned, they weren't rehearsed, and they weren't words I had ever imagined saying. But they were so fuckin' true that my eyes stung with tears.

"You're falling in love with me?" Kennedy's tears spilled over, and his face filled with a goofy smile.

I laughed. "Yeah. I have nothing to compare it to, but…I'm pretty sure I am."

"That's a good thing."

"Yeah?" I raised a brow.

"Mmhm, 'cause I'm pretty sure I'm falling in love with you, too. And I don't know if I could handle being the only one to feel that way." Kennedy leaned in to kiss me. "This way we can be unsure together."

"Perfect plan." I whispered against his lips. "Now, let's get some sleep. We have a whole day of lounging in bed tomorrow."

"Only lounging?" Kennedy bit his lip.

"Well, if we're doing more than lounging then we definitely need some sleep." I kissed his nose before tucking him back into my arms to cuddle into my chest. "G'night."

"G'night. Love you." Kennedy whispered and my heart swelled.

"Love you, too."

Chapter 16

Kennedy

I woke early, but when I realized I was safe and warm in Cody's arms and had nowhere to be, I fell back to sleep.

When ten o'clock came into focus the second time I woke, I was shocked I'd slept so late. Cody's arms were still locked around me, but I didn't feel trapped or bound. Quite the opposite, although Cody was holding me, I felt more like he was using me as his anchor and his safe spot. The man was in control of every aspect of his life, but deep down he wanted so badly to let go.

And it looked like I was the lucky one to help him let go.

But was I enough? I had practically zero control of most of my life. Was I man enough to be what Cody needed?

"What are you thinking about?" Cody's sleep roughened voice murmured in my ear.

"Just thinking about the sides we present to the world and the roles we naturally fall into in comparison with the sides our bodies and hearts seem to want to take us." The words came so easily when speaking with Cody.

"And?"

"And what?" I turned in his arms to see him better.

"I feel there's more," Cody prodded.

I shrugged. "Just wondering if I'm enough to take you where you want to go. I want nothing more than to control you and own you and command you. But sometimes I wonder if I'm just kidding myself. Look at me, I'm not exactly the stereotypical dominant."

"I love looking at you," Cody growled before kissing me deeply then pulling back. "Our physical features have nothing to do with our relationship or where we'd like to see it go." He ran a hand down my arm before palming my ass. "I plan to have this ass on my tongue and around my cock," his hand traveled to grip my morning wood, "just as much as I pray I'll get to have this cock down my throat and pounding into my ass."

I shivered and pumped into his hand. "I have no issue with any of that."

"I guess what I'm trying to say is that our wants and roles in this relationship aren't something I see as concrete." Cody nuzzled my neck and continued to stroke my cock. "Desires are very fluid for many people. We may want soft and slow, hard and fast, simple and easy, or kinky and playful. All of those wants can change from day to day. There are no hard and fast rules here. We have nothing to prove to anyone."

"I like that." I reached to cup his ass. "I guess I've been pigeonholed into the bottom and submissive position so often, I fell into the same stereotyping I was a victim of. But, you're right." With my index finger, I teased along Cody's crack until I reached his balls. "And as much as I dream of owning every single inch of you and fucking you until you're begging for release, I dream just as much of getting that beautiful dick back in *my* ass."

"And doing it right this time?"

I chuckled. "It wasn't wrong last time. We just still sort of hated each other. More is at stake now and emotions are involved. I think it will be different."

"You think you can fuck me until I'm begging in the shower, or are you going to need breakfast first?" Cody's question came with promise and challenge.

"I think a shower will suffice. But you need to watch that cheeky little mouth of yours." I gripped a globe of Cody's perfect ass in my hand.

"First, there's nothing *little* about me." Cody punctuated his comment with a thrust of his cock into mine. "Second, just what are *you* going to do about my mouth?"

God how my blood boiled when Cody got mouthy. "I think a good mouth fucking would be a good start. But a mouth like yours likely needs a gag while I give your ass a thorough fucking."

Cody whimpered into my neck, but his words came out strong. "I'd like to see you try."

"Shower. Now."

I gave Cody time in the bathroom by himself. When he emerged, I shouldered past him and nodded my head to the bed. "Left some things for you. I want you in them when I come out."

Cody's gaze traveled over the bed and his nostrils flared. "We'll see," he clipped out, but he bit his lip and his breath seemed to increase.

Ten minutes later, after the quickest shower I'd likely ever taken, I walked into the bedroom with only a towel around my waist and then nearly fell to my knees. Cody was sprawled on the bed, a black leather harness framing his broad chest, a silver chain trailing down his torso until it reached a black leather cock ring wrapped around his cock and balls.

I dropped the towel and made my way to the bed's edge while admiring the man laid out before me. I reached for the leather flogger and leaned down to kiss the leaking head of Cody's dick. Licking the pre-cum and swirling my tongue around the tight skin, I groaned before trailing kisses up his abs until I reached his mouth. "Best thing I've ever seen in my bed. Ever." I nibbled at Cody's lips and licked away what I hoped was a sting he'd feel all the way to his core. "One of my first dreams about you had you in a harness and cock ring. We definitely need a ball gag and nipple rings to make my dreams come true." I pulled on the harness and rolled him to his side before I brought the flogger down on Cody's ass.

My balls tightened when he gasped as the leather strips met his skin.

The way his skin immediately pinked was enough to make me almost come all over myself, but I gripped my balls and dug through the side table's drawer for another cock ring.

"Do it again," Cody begged with his ass in the air, his hands clasped on his bowed head, and his dick jutting proudly from his body.

"Do what?" I demanded.

"Whip me, spank me, whatever you want to call it. Just do it."

"Pretty sure I'm the one in control here. I'll give you what you want when you work for it. I want you begging." I climbed behind him and immediately devoured his puckered hole with my lips and probing tongue. "I think you need prepped. Reach into that drawer for a plug."

"No, I can take it, please."

I smacked my hand down on Cody's ass. Hard. "I said, pick out a butt plug."

Cody started to reach for his cock, but I slapped his ass again. "You can touch yourself when I tell you to. Get the plug."

Cody turned desire-filled eyes my way and jutted out his chin.

"If you don't obey, I'll make it worse until you do. Your ass is so damn tight. I could barely push in my tongue. You need stretched before my cock gets in there." I slapped his ass before running a soothing palm over the handprint. "I'll let you suck me while you adjust to the plug."

Once Cody had a plug, I reached for the lube.

After dribbling the liquid around his hole, I poured some over the shiny black butt plug. "You ready, baby?" I teased Cody's hole with the tip of the silicone.

Cody pressed his ass against the plug. "Yes," he hissed, "just do it."

I watched in apt fascination as his body opened to take the plug. "God, just imagine when this is my cock. Will you open for me? Squeeze me like you're doing now?"

Cody grunted and tried to stroke himself.

Once the plug was snuggly in place, I climbed from the bed and stood next to the mattress. Pressing Cody to his side, I pulled him close by the harness.

"Suck me." The command sent shivers through me, and Cody's glassy eyes heated at the demand.

He opened his mouth and greedily tongued my head before sucking me deep.

I gripped his head and pumped into his hot mouth several times before I realized I'd be done too soon if I didn't stop. Pulling away, I rolled him to his back and joined him on the bed again. His fat cock teased me, red and pulsing, his balls drawn up tight in the leather band. I leaned in to kiss his swollen lips, licking the taste of me from his mouth, and then reached to stroke his hard length.

"God, don't. I can't take it." Cody whimpered against my mouth. "I wanna come. Need to come. Please, fuck me."

"Shhhh, baby. I've got you." I whispered before devouring his mouth. "Be patient. I'm going to pull that plug from your ass in just a minute and slide my cock in deep. I'll fuck your ass so hard."

Cody trembled and groaned.

"You like that, baby? You want me to fuck that pretty ass of yours?" I rolled him from his back to his side again so we were chest to chest. I brought my hand down hard on his perfect bubble butt over and over until he cried out. Capturing his mouth in mine as I caressed his red, welted skin. "Tell me, baby. Tell me what you want."

"You. I want you in me. Spank me, fuck me, and fill me. I want your body in mine." Cody pulled me in for a voracious, desperate kiss. "Please."

I rolled him to his stomach. "On your knees, ass up." While I watched him comply with my commands, I rolled a condom down my dick.

Cody shivered as I teased the plug out, in, and back again. The moment his ass was free of the silicone, I took my place behind him and pressed firmly against his hole.

"Relax, baby. Push against me." I eased my way past the first ring of muscle.

Cody hissed through his teeth.

"Take me, baby. Open for me." I pushed in the rest of the way and simply held myself in position until Cody's body adjusted to my cock. "You okay?"

"Yeah," Cody gasped.

I reached for the harness and pulled his back up to my chest, knowing the chain between the harness and cock ring would bring a pleasurable pain. I had Cody in the exact position as the first time I'd ever imagined topping him. "Put your arms back and hold on."

Cody reached around to grip my ass. "Fuck me, please."

Never before had anyone begged me to take them, to fuck them, or to own their ass. Harness held tight, I pumped hard and deep into Cody's perfect ass. The sight of his pink skin jiggling with each thrust brought me to release. I roared and filled the condom with wet, hot pulses. "Jack yourself." I popped the snap on the leather cock ring.

With my dick still pulsing in his ass, my hand still tight on the harness, Cody stroked himself to completion before collapsing when I let go of the harness.

Once I'd disposed of the condom, I joined the breathless, motionless heap of man.

We laid together for several moments before I finally gathered the energy and courage to speak. "Was that okay?"

Cody chuckled and moved so he could pull me into his arms. "I actually have no words for how fucking okay that was."

I sighed. "So, we can definitely do that and more again?"

"Fuck, yes."

"But," I hedged and bit my lip.

Cody pulled back and looked at me. "But what? Did you not enjoy it?"

"No, it was fucking fantastic. Beyond the best I've ever had," I assured him.

"So, but, what?"

"I'm a little jealous of your spanking and leather and fucking." I knew I was blushing. "Can we switch it up soon?"

Cody laughed and pulled me close to kiss my head. "Why did we waste so much time hating each other when we could have been fucking and loving each other? We damn sure can."

I smiled into Cody's chest. "Let's sleep. We can do brunch later."

"Sounds good."

Cody tucked me into the space of his arms and chest, and we were soon both sound asleep.

~~*

"How long have you been awake?" Cody grumbled and hid his face in the pillow when he woke to find me watching him.

"A while. I've been thinking."

Cody peeked at me from the pillow. "About?"

"Why we hate each other."

"Pretty sure we don't hate each other." Cody smirked. "But, I'd be happy for an encore performance if you need persuading."

I cocked a brow. "First, people who hate each other have sex all the time. That's not the point. Second, you know what I meant. I figured out why we used to hate each other."

Cody propped up on an elbow. "You've got my attention. Go ahead."

"We wanted to be each other," I said with a shrug.

"Huh?" Cody curled up his nose.

"Think about it." I leaned closer. "Deep down inside, I want to take control, dominate, and own you. Deep down inside, you wanted to *be* controlled, dominated, and owned. Those feelings were new and unfamiliar. So, instead of dealing with the feelings that rattled us and made us uncomfortable, we put up our defenses. It was easier to hate and lash out than to admit what we wanted."

Cody stared at me for several moments. "Well, I'll be damned." He frowned. "So, why the change?"

"Think about it. Jay locked us up together. We were forced to interact. We had sex and both recognized it wasn't as great as it could have been. The seed was planted and put down deep roots." I gestured between the two of us. "Over time, as we got to know each other better, it was easier to accept the feelings, easier to admit the desires, and here we are."

Cody dropped his head face first into the pillow and groaned.

"Um, is this bad news?"

"Yes, it's terrible news." Cody's voice was muffled into the fluff.

"Oh, um…I'm sorry." I wracked my brain trying to figure out why Cody was distressed. "It's just a theory, probably not even right."

"No, it sounds spot on." Cody rolled so his mouth wasn't covered by the pillow. "By the way, did you minor in psychology or something? You're all sexy and shit when you're psychoanalyzing our relationship."

I smirked and felt my cheeks heat. "So, why are you upset? Why is this a bad thing? I thought it would help to figure out our hatred and eventual crossover."

"Because, damn it…" Cody rubbed a hand over his face, and I held my breath in dreaded anticipation. "It means that *Jay* got us together. Nothing worse than having to admit that little shit was right." Cody tried to keep a straight face.

I smacked his shoulder. "You ass! I thought you were really mad."

"I am!" Cody insisted. "I hate thinking Jay's little plot worked exactly the way he planned."

I sobered for a moment. "So, you'd rather we never got locked in the basement? Never crossed that fine line between hate and love?" My heart hurt. "You'd rather Jay be wrong than us be happy?"

Cody paused and then pulled me close for a kiss. "Not on your life." His mouth devoured mine then eased away. "I'll tell the entire world Jay was right if I have to. I hate to admit *to Jay* that he was right, but I'll spend the rest of my life grateful that little shit locked me in the basement with you."

I smiled wide into the next kiss, our teeth bumping. "Agreed. Putting up with Jay's gloating is worth it." I pulled from the kiss slightly. "And, I have to say, I'm so much happier loving you than hating you. Hating you was exhausting torture."

Cody cocked his head to the side and was quiet for a moment. "You know, you're right. I wasn't *un*happy before, but things just feel better, more *right* than ever before, now that I can openly like you than instead of portraying my hatred for you day in and day out."

"I totally get that." I kissed his cheek. "Want some breakfast? Pretty sure my kitchen isn't as stocked as Jay's basement, but I bet we can stir up something." My stomach growled as I spoke.

Cody and I both laughed.

"Yes, I'm starving."

Ten minutes later, I waited for the waffle iron to heat after mixing up waffle batter. "Can I ask something?" My heart pounded, not sure the bright light of my kitchen the morning after my emotional breakdown and our mind-blowing sex was the best place for this conversation, but I couldn't stop myself.

Cody cocked a brow and waited.

"So, what are we doing?"

"Making waffles." Cody deadpanned.

I huffed and rolled my eyes. "You know what I mean." I tested the waffle iron with a drop of batter. It sizzled as a sign it was ready so I poured on the batter. "Playing? Serious? Hookup? Friends with benefits?" I turned a solemn eye toward Cody. "I'll deal with whatever our label, but I really need to know where we stand."

Cody's brow furrowed before he grabbed my hips and pulled me close. "Sort of thought the events of the last twelve hours spoke for themselves. But if you need words and details, I can do that." He leaned in and kissed my forehead, my nose, and then my lips. "I don't tell hookups or friends with benefits or play things I love them. I've *never* told anyone I love them." He kissed me again. "I've never offered my body to another like I did for you. And I take the words and the actions *very* seriously."

"So if someone were to ask what we are to each other?" My eyes stung with unshed tears.

"You're burning the waffles," Cody quipped.

"Damn it," I gasped and turned to remove the waffles from the iron. "Stop avoiding the question."

"Fine," Cody huffed dramatically. "I guess I would call us partners? Boyfriends? Committed?" His cheeks flushed as he ducked his chin to his chest and glanced my way. "If you're okay with that?"

I couldn't help the huge smile that took up half my face. "I guess I'm okay with that." I tried to play nonchalant.

"Oh, you *guess*? Just *okay* with it, huh?" Cody teased and pulled me back to his chest for a full-body hug. "Damn, I love you. I'm sorry I wasted so much time thinking I hated you." He kissed the top of my head.

"It's okay." I snuggled into him. "Maybe we weren't ready for anything before now." I thought about the two of us. "Honestly, I think maybe the long standing hatred made this better. It's more appreciated. Means more?"

"Yeah, maybe you're right." Cody let me go so he could fill the iron with more waffle batter. "Slather some butter on those."

"Can I ask another question?" I smeared butter on the waffles.

"Gee, inquisitive this morning, huh?" Cody winked. "Of course."

"I know you've had a third and maybe even a fourth join in from time to time when you're playing. Is that something you want with me?"

Cody paused, started to speak, paused again. And frowned.

"A third is always fun," he spoke slowly and watched my face, "but I can honestly say that I'm not ready to share you at this point. If that's okay with you?"

I smiled. "I'm not against a third at some point, but this is all so new right now. I'd like to just keep it to us. Maybe further down the road, when things are more cemented, but I like the idea of just the two of us for now, too."

"What if one of us never wants to add a third or a fourth?" Cody cocked his head and waited.

"I think it's a conversation we have when that time comes." I rubbed my chin. "Until then, we keep communication open, but no invitations given unless we mutually agree later in the relationship."

"I'm good with that." Cody smiled and slid more waffles onto a plate.

We settled at the table with buttery waffles soaked in syrup and powdered sugar.

"Let's play a game," Cody suggested.

I stopped with my waffle-filled fork midway to my mouth. "Kind of busy here."

"You can eat as we play." Cody walked to the counter and got two pages of notebook paper and two pens. "Left side is for hard limits. Right side is for ready/open/willing to try."

My cock hardened just thinking of all the things I was ready and willing to try with Cody. I slashed a line down the middle of my paper and went to work making my list.

Fifteen minutes later, waffles gone, dishes washed, and lists completed, we sat back down at the table. In a move worthy of a Hollywood drama, we swapped lists.

My heart beat faster as I read through Cody's list and realized our hard limits were almost identical. It wouldn't have been a deal breaker, but having similar hard limits was helpful. And almost like fate had a hand in it.

Shit. I was ready to get started on the open and willing list. Like, *now*. I glanced up to catch Cody's heated gaze upon me and knew he was just as ready.

"This will be fun." I waggled my brow.

"You can say that again." Cody winked. "I think we need to stock up at the next Leather Sunday if we plan to work our way through these lists."

"I'm game." Hell, was it Sunday yet? I scanned the list again. "I think we have access to some of these with items already."

"Agreed." Cody nodded. "When are you off for a couple days?"

"I'll have to make up for calling off today. But, I should have two or three days in a row next week."

"Okay, Leather Sunday we stock up. Then we head up to Indy for a little road trip vacay." Cody raised a brow. "You down with that?"

"One hundred percent."

CHAPTER 17

CODY

I worked the room in my jeans, boots, and leather harness, chatting with the regulars, making sure the newbies were comfortable, and checking on drinks.

Music pumped, and the air was heavy with leather, musk, beer, and the scent of men.

Leather Sunday always sparked a fire in me, but this one seemed to be stoking a roaring inferno. I caught Kennedy at the display table in his black jeans, boots, vest, and sir cap. It was the first Leather Sunday he'd switched up his gear and donned the cap. He'd gotten plenty of second glances. Maybe it was my imagination, but I got the impression there were quite a few disappointed men. Disappointed that he wasn't an available sub. Disappointed that he wasn't looking to hook up. He was very clearly with me. It made my heart swell and my cock harden.

When he turned and caught me staring, he winked. I knew he was perusing the items we would be taking home.

"Don't want to interrupt your ogling," Dad spoke at my side, "but the Stringer lady is outside screaming obscenities."

"Let her scream for now. The event is well under way. I doubt anyone else is coming. I'll have Kennedy call the police department before everyone leaves." I watched Kennedy deep in conversation with the retailer across the room. Vicki Stringer was a nuisance, but I had no intention of letting her mess with what I had.

Dad nodded and headed to refill drinks. I had to laugh at his ease around all the leather-clad bodies. Dad was a hard worker and a businessman at heart. He knew Leather Sunday brought in a ton of business and money. He judged people based on how they treated him and others. He may not have any interest in the leather scene, and he was definitely going home to Mom, but he took to Leather Sundays like a fish to water.

"Officer Kinky has quite the assortment of toys over there." Jay hung on Levi's arm and pointed toward Kennedy. "I saw a plug, a gag, nipple clamps, bindings, and a cage." Jay waggled his brow. "Who's the cage for? I don't see that as an individual purchase. Which cock is getting locked up?"

I rolled my eyes even as I felt heat rush up my cheeks. "Not mine," I scoffed.

"Mmmhm," Jay hummed and Levi smirked.

"Go get kinky," I ordered.

"Why? It's fun giving you a hard time and watching you blush." Jay batted his purple-mascaraed lashes.

"Seriously, go away." I wiped a table before tossing the towel behind the bar. "The entertainment starts soon. I want to get a decent seat." I turned toward Kennedy and left Jay and Levi laughing behind me.

"But, talking to *you* was so entertaining!" Jay hollered after me.

I reached Kennedy as he was accepting his plain brown paper bag from the man behind the display table. "You ready to find a seat?" I took his elbow and nuzzled against his neck.

"Yep." Kennedy shook the bag. "Can I put this in the office?"

I nodded and watched as Kennedy sauntered to the back. Maybe it was because I was looking at him in a totally different light these days, but I swear he positively owned the place with the confidence he exuded.

"Been watching you two for a quite a while." The man behind the table smirked while he arranged the items on display. "Wondered when you'd finally get your heads from your asses and get together."

I started to argue, to defend, to tell him it really wasn't his business, but I stopped. I chuckled. "Yeah, took us long enough, but we had to do it our own way."

The man nodded. "He sure was eyeing the cock cages."

"Not sure we're at that point." I hedged as I glanced at the different cages on the table. Silicone, metal, smooth, spikes, locks, keys. I wasn't sure if the rush traveling through my body was nausea from uncertainty or desire from anticipation.

"Well, you let me know if you ever decide you *are* at that point." The man gave me a final nod as Kennedy returned and the entertainment took the stage. *Stage* was a loose term for the area we'd cleared toward the front. I prayed the temporary poles we'd allowed the group to install would hold throughout their show.

"How the hell do they *do* that?" Levi marveled as the three men totally worked it on the poles. "I mean, the rhythm, the flexibility, the exhibition, it's an all an art form in and of itself."

Jay frowned, pouting his lip out. "Well, I mean, I guess if you like *that* type of thing."

Levi laughed and pulled Jay to his side. "No worries, baby. I prefer your private dances to this. I'm just impressed by how they put it all together."

"Oh!" Jay pulled away and clapped his hands together. "Let's take a BJ Boys trip to learn pole dancing!"

"No," Levi, Kennedy, and I all stated at once.

"Not a chance," Micah added flatly. By his side, Cole shook his head.

Jay huffed. "Fine. *I'll* learn pole dancing. But don't think I'll show it to any of you." Jay jabbed his finger at most of us, but turned a sultry smile toward Levi. "Daddy, can I have a pole in the basement?"

Levi turned to watch the men gyrating on the poles on stage before turning back to Jay. "You can have any damn thing in the basement you want."

Jay preened and batted his lashes. "Thank you. Your private showing will debut soon."

Levi growled and pulled Jay into a bear hug. "Can't wait."

Before the show was over, I told Kennedy about Vicki being outside.

When the pole dancing ended, Kennedy checked his phone. "Captain says Stringer has been taken care of. He sent a couple officers to run her off. Should be safe to let the patrons leave."

"Great. Thanks." I kissed him soundly. "I gotta stay and clean up. Don't wait for me. I know you've got work."

"Would love to hang around and help, but I'm beat." Kennedy wrapped me tightly in his arms. "I'll text you when I'm sure of my schedule. Still want to head to Indy?"

"Definitely. Let me know, and I'll work it out with my schedule here."

Kennedy kissed along my jawline before whispering in my ear. "Sounds good. Love you."

"Love you, too." I kissed him one last time before turning away and running smack dab into a beaming Jay.

"Oh. My. God." Jay clapped his hands and bounced on his toes. "I knew it! You two are in love! I want your butt babies to be named after me! Jayson, Jaylene, Tee-Jay, Emjay…we can work on the names." He clutched Levi's arm. "Daddy, did you see them? Did you hear them? They love each other! My plan worked!"

"The way Cody is working his jaw, I'm guessing you might want to take your excitement down about ten notches on the celebration scale." Levi smirked and winked at me.

As much as it pained me to tell Jay he was right, I pulled Kennedy close to my side. "You guys already knew we're together, and yes, I love him."

Jay's eyes glazed over with unshed tears, and he bit his lip.

"And, yes, your prison plot set things into motion." I turned and kissed the top of Kennedy's head when he laid it on my shoulder. "But, I'm gonna need you to tone it down and get the gloating out of your system as soon as fucking possible. Got it?"

Jay nodded happily. "I can do that."

Kennedy and I watched as Levi dragged a teary-eye Jay out the door.

"Well, I guess he's happy." Kennedy chuckled.

"Yeah, seems like it." I rolled my eyes. Pulling Kennedy back for one last kiss, I smiled. "And I am, too. Love you. Sleep tight and work safe."

"You, too," Kennedy whispered into my mouth before deepening the kiss.

I pushed him away with a grin. "Go on. Get out of here before I ruin you for your shift."

"Maybe I want to be ruined." Kennedy winked. "Or perhaps I should work on ruining *you*?"

One last kiss and I sent him out the door before turning to finish the clean up.

"Hey, man. Let me help you with packing up," I hollered at the man boxing up the display table. "Dad, can you take care of the tables?"

Dad nodded.

Within an hour, Leather Sunday was packed away for another week and the B & B was ready for Monday brunch.

~~*

"What's all that?" I asked Kennedy when he tossed his duffel bag and a grocery bag into the backseat of my truck when I picked him up.

"Snacks," Kennedy replied with a smile as he climbed into the truck. "Can't drive over two hours to Indy without provisions."

I grinned. "What did you bring?"

Kennedy reached for the bag and began searching through it. "Chips, chocolate, Red Vines, pistachios, cashews, and Nerds."

"Good Lord, man. How old are you?" I dug into the bag and grabbed a Red Vine from the package Kennedy had obviously already torn into. "You're set for a road trip like a thirteen-year-old kid."

"Have to have the sweet and salty bases covered," Kennedy pointed out.

"Well, you did a good job." I eased onto the exit leaving Blueridge Junction to head north toward Indianapolis.

"I don't see you complaining." Kennedy smacked me with a Red Vine. "By the way, I feel our relationship is fated because we both like Red Vines."

"Nothing better than *real* red licorice." I gestured with the shiny red vine in my hand.

"So, I trust you're not a Twizzlers fan?" Kennedy cocked his head as if my answer held the weight of the world.

"Eeew, no. Twizzlers are disgusting." I curled my nose.

"Thank you!" Kennedy chomped down on his candy. "Can we stop to get drinks?"

"Yeah, I was thinking maybe swinging through a Starbucks?" I glanced toward Kennedy.

"Perfect."

"So, I booked us a room." I reached for Kennedy's hand. "Union Station."

"Cool, I've never been to Union Station. Actually, been a while since I've been to Indy." Kennedy popped some cashews in his mouth.

"Levi said we should check out Metro for drinks and dinner." I'd already checked out the place online and liked the look of it.

"Sounds good."

The drive north was filled with comfortable chitchat and equally comfortable silence as we snacked, sipped our Starbucks, and listened to whatever radio station came in.

By the time we reached the city, I needed to piss and stretch my legs. We took Madison Avenue to South Street before turning north on Illinois and arrived at Union Station. "I'll make sure we're checked in and see where to park. You good to stay here? Move the car if a traffic cop comes by?"

"Sure," Kennedy smirked. "Hate it when those damn cops try to enforce the law."

I rolled my eyes. "Shut it."

Within fifteen minutes, we were checked in, parked and heading up the elevator to our room. I felt like a giddy kid with a surprise waiting. We headed down the long hallway, room doors to our left and old train cars to our right.

"Whoa, those are cool." Kennedy slowed to stare at the train cars. "Think they are authentic?"

I kept walking until I saw our room. "Guess we'll find out." I pointed toward the steps leading up to the car. "That one's ours."

"What?" Kennedy's eyes grew wide. "In the *train*?"

"Yep." I grinned. "Go on. Climb up."

We walked into a very narrow room, but the fact we were rooming *in* a train car was beyond cool. The room was skinny, but it had a bed, television, bathroom, fridge, and everything a normal hotel room would have.

"This is the coolest thing I've ever seen." Kennedy tossed his bag of snacks and overnight bag on the bed and explored the room.

My heart swelled with delight to know Kennedy was as pleased and excited about our room as I was.

"There's a pool if we decide to swim." I grabbed a map of the hotel.

Kennedy browsed the information brochure. "No way," he whispered.

"What?"

"Stories in here about haunted train cars." Kennedy returned to reading. "Holy shit. That's enough to give a person the creeps for sure."

"Seriously? Haunted?" I moved to read with him. "Whoa, yeah. That gives me chills."

"Swear to God, if we wake to creepy shit tonight, I can't promise I won't beat the shit out of you in fear." Kennedy laughed.

"Same."

Kennedy stood and shivered. "Let's explore the city. I think a lot of things are within walking distance."

"Take your jacket. It's a decent day, but when the sun goes down it will be chilly." I tossed his jacket through the air before walking closer and grabbing him by the waist. "You happy with it? The trip? The room?"

Kennedy's face softened and his beautiful smile glowed. "Baby, I'd be happy in the guest house with carry-out. But, yes, this trip and this room are amazing. Thank you." He leaned in and kissed me. "Getting out of town and relaxing is just what I needed. Doing it all with you makes it even better."

We spent the next several hours walking the city like complete tourists. Indianapolis was aesthetically pleasing, easy to navigate, as friendly as one could expect in a large city, and full of history.

"Let's do Metro tomorrow. We can hit it for dinner and hang around for drinks." Kennedy rested his head on my shoulder as we walked around

Monument Circle. "Honestly, I'm too tired for a bar scene right now."

"No problem." I kissed his head. "Want to do the Old Spaghetti Factory for supper? Then we can look for something else to do or just hang out in the room."

"Mmm, spaghetti sounds fabulous. And, honestly, the thought of cuddling in bed is top of my list right now."

The Old Spaghetti Factory was delicious, beautiful, and a hell of a lot of food for a great price. Kennedy thumbed through a ghost story book he'd picked up at a bookstore on our walk.

"Oh my god, supposedly there's a ghost here in this restaurant." Kennedy read a bit before speaking again. "Says this building used to be a shoe factory and supposedly a little girl died working in it. People say they've seen a little girl, especially in the basement, and then she disappears."

"Aren't the restrooms in the basement?"

"Yeah, I think so," Kennedy murmured.

"I don't think I'll use the restroom here." I laughed and ate another piece of warm bread.

"Man, there are *a lot* of ghost stories about this city." Kennedy continued to read. "We should come back sometime, maybe when it's warmer, and take one of the haunted walking tours."

"That would be great. Definitely a plan."

We finished dinner, complete with spumoni for dessert, and headed out for a chilly walk back to our room.

"I want a warm shower and nothing but bed," Kennedy spoke through a yawn.

"I'm down with that." Indianapolis would forever be in my heart and mind as the first trip Kennedy and I took together. And the city where I fell in love with him even more.

Kennedy snuggled in my arms as we watched whatever random movie happened to be on the TV.

I was warm and drowsy from my shower. "You want to make it an early night?" I whispered to the top of Kennedy's head, wondering if he was already asleep.

He lifted his head, eyes sleepy, but I saw a gleam in them. "Not really. Unless you're too tired?"

"Nah, I'm good. What did you have in mind?" I kissed his cheek and nuzzled my nose at his temple.

"Remember when we talked about our desires and roles being fluid?"

I nodded.

"I'm feeling like soft and slow may be perfect for tonight." Kennedy bit his lip. "And I was kinda hoping you'd want to be the one doing me soft and slow?"

I smirked. "Don't want it hard and fast and kinky in the train car?"

Kennedy pushed up on his arms. "Just so you know, I always do and always will want it any and every way you want to give it or take it."

I smiled bigger. "Good to know."

Kennedy shrugged. "I'm just feeling the need to be under you tonight."

"Just so *you* know. I always do and always will want it any and every way you want to give or take it."

Kennedy chuckled. "Good to know."

I rolled him to his back, stripped the clothing from his body, and trailed kisses from his lips to his toes and back. The slight dimple in his chin, the dusty peaks of his nipples, and the promising trail of soft hair down his abdomen. Stopping to lick and play with his cock before heading to nip at his inner thighs and then down to nibble his toes.

Kennedy rolled to grab lube and a condom from his duffle at the side of the bed.

"What would you think of getting tested and doing this without the condoms?" I spoke the words before I even thought them through.

He simply nodded and pulled me in for a slow kiss. Kennedy turned to roll to his hands and knees, but I stopped him.

"I want you on your back." I trailed my hands down his torso, gripping his hips, and spreading his legs so that my hips could fit snuggly between. Reaching to wrap his legs around my waist, I leaned down on my elbows and studied his face.

Kennedy's eyes widened.

"Is that okay?"

His eyes filled with tears and my heart sank.

"If you don't like it that way, it's okay."

"No," Kennedy shook his head, "it's just I've never had sex like this."

I cocked my head. "You know, I don't know that I ever had either. I've taken guys on their back, but it's usually with their legs thrown over my shoulders." I glanced down to admire how our bodies looked in such an intimate position. "This seems right though."

Kennedy nodded. "It does. It's emotional, seems more real, more like love rather than just sex."

I held his hands in mine up by his shoulders as I rocked slowly against him. "Baby, I don't know that anything between us will *ever* be just sex." Hovering my lips over his mouth, I continued, "Probably because when I take you this way, I plan on you knowing the depth of my love in every cell of your body."

Making quick work of the condom and lube, I returned to my position between his legs.

Inching my hard length into Kennedy's ass slowly, I held my breath and bit my lip until his body gave way and accepted me completely. Softly and slowly, I pumped deeply into his body. "Never been this good," I whispered harshly. Truly, I'd never felt such an intimate connection to anyone in my entire life.

The extreme pleasure of making love to Kennedy lasted for several minutes until he locked his legs around my waist and cried my name as he shot ropes of white between our bodies.

As his body clutched mine, I filled the condom and buried my head at Kennedy's ear. "So damn good. Fuck, I love you."

Sleep came quick and easy after a wipe down. Holding Kennedy in my arms, my body still shaking from release, I knew I'd found what had been missing.

CHAPTER 18

KENNEDY

Never in my life had anyone *made love* to me. I never knew the difference. Never knew it was something I'd enjoy. Something I'd crave with every ounce of my being. Having Cody make love to me while whispering his love was as much a turn on as owning him and making him submit to me.

I woke in the middle of the night after several hours of sleep. I rolled Cody to his back and settled between his legs as he emerged from slumber. "I want my turn."

Cody growled and pulled me in for a deep kiss. "And I want mine."

I donned a condom before spreading the slick lube along my dick and Cody's ass. "You okay with it this way?"

Cody nodded, but he put his hands against my chest. "I need you to know that giving myself to you through the kink and play is real and true and wanted." He gritted his teeth, his jaw bulging. "But this? I've never been so open and raw with anyone in my entire life."

My heart caught in my chest, and I pressed against his arms until they gave way and I could reach his mouth. "And I love you even harder than ever before because of it." I kissed him, breathing deeply of our mixed scents. "I cherish this and will honor it with every part of my soul."

"Make love to me," Cody whispered.

"Always." I pressed at his body, my throbbing dick begging for entry into his tight heat. "Relax for me, baby." When his tight ring stretched to allow me to sink deep, I had to hold myself still for several seconds. "Fuuuck."

Cody wrapped his legs around my waist, and he locked his arms around my torso.

I pumped into his body with small, but firm, thrusts and kept his dick trapped tight between our bodies.

Framing his face with my hands, I lost myself in his bright gaze. "I love you, Cody. Love you, love your body, love your desires, and love your heart." When a tear escaped from the corner of his eye, I leaned in quickly to kiss it away. "Come for me, baby. I want to feel your ass clench around me, milk me, make us sticky."

Cody's body shook under me, his head thrown back as he groaned my name and painted his release onto both our skins. Pulling from his body as far as his arms and legs would allow, I thrust one last time before spilling into the condom.

Collapsing my full weight on Cody, I allowed my tears to mix with his as we held each other with trembling arms for several minutes.

"Baby?" Cody mumbled into my neck.

"Mmmm?"

"I gotta pee. And if we don't shower soon, we'll be stuck together like glue."

I chuckled. "Okay, okay. Quick shower and then a little more sleep before day two of touring the city. That work?"

"Perfect." Cody kissed me.

Fifteen minutes later, we were back in bed, curled in each other's arms.

"Thank you," Cody whispered.

"Same." I smiled into the dark. "I love you."

"Same." He tightened his arms around me.

~~*

Our second, and last, day in Indy was just as spectacular as the first. The city really was an enjoyable place to be. There were great small business shops and restaurants, fun bars and restaurants, museums, and some interesting history to read up on. Cody and I decided we'd definitely make trips to Indianapolis a regular thing. We'd meant to make it to Metro, a gay bar Levi had suggested, among other places, but we never did. Just another reason for other trips. We ended our second day with room service, a sensual shower, and an early night knowing we had to get up early to make the drive back to BJ.

"Rise and shine," Cody grumbled after he'd hit snooze on his alarm.

We dozed in bed for several moments before truly stirring to begin the process of waking, showering, and packing up.

"You want to eat before we leave town? Or grab something on the road?" I ran a towel through my hair after showering.

"I'm good with stopping somewhere farther south." Cody turned off the shower and climbed out.

In twenty minutes, we were packed and ready, but Cody was hem-hawing around, all twitchy like.

"You okay?" I cocked a brow.

"Huh?" Cody whipped his gaze toward me. "Oh, yeah, I'm good."

"Ready to go?"

"Um, no." Cody ran his palms down the front of his jeans. "Can you, um, just sit on the bed for a second?"

"What's wrong?" I worried my lip.

"Nothing. It's good. We're good." Cody rummaged in his duffel while I settled on the side of the bed to wait.

He pulled a brown paper bag from his duffel and sat in the desk chair.

"So, um, I got you something. Or *us*. I guess I got us something." He thrust the bag at me.

I frowned and laughed, sounding just as nervous as I felt. Wondering what the hell had Cody acting so weird, I dug into the bag and came out with a soft leather pouch.

"Open it," Cody encouraged with a nod of his head.

Loosening the strings on the pouch, I poured the contents into my hand. Smooth resin plopped into my hand and felt cool against my skin for a brief moment before my body heat began to warm it. The tinkling of two small keys falling from the bag followed. My head jerked up to meet Cody's gaze. "A chastity cage?" I turned the metal cage over in my hand and fingered the small key attached to the locking device.

Cody chewed at his bottom lip.

"For me?"

"For you in that *I'm* going to wear it. I want you to put it on me."

"But why?" I crinkled my brow. "Not that I'm not about to bust a nut over this, don't get me wrong."

"Remember when you said you wanted to own me? Cage me? Wanted my pain and pleasure to belong to you?"

I nodded.

"I want that, too."

"But, you didn't seem to gung-ho on the idea." The smooth resin continued to heat in my hand. "And at Leather Sunday you seemed pretty put off by the cage display."

"Proof that a man can change his mind." Cody leaned forward, elbows on knees. "The thought of wearing this for you, only you and I knowing I have it on, is like white hot flames licking at my balls." He reached for the keys and toyed with them between his fingers. "Will you be my key holder?"

Part of me wanted to strip Cody, slap the cage on him, and hide the key. I frowned. The other part of me needed to know this was what Cody wanted. "I would love to. But I need to know this is for you as much as it is for me."

Cody nodded. "Figured you would." He stared at the key while he spoke. "This cage means several things for me. One, it means giving up control. That's something I'm not very good at, but it's something I want. It also means you own me, through the pleasure and the pain, the ups and the downs." Cody chuckled at his unintended innuendo. "Part of this cage allows me to be a greedy, hungry little slut. That's something I've *never* been, but god I want it with you." He held the keys up again. "Knowing you wear this key around your neck or in your pocket while I can't get off unless you allow it? That gives me such an incredible rush. I don't even know if I can explain it."

I took a deep breath as I processed his words. "Wow, I'm touched."

"If it's too much, I understand," Cody muttered.

"No," I reached for the key, "it's not too much. Yes, it's a lot, but in a good way." I studied the cage in my hand. "I think you should keep one of the keys at your place. Just in case of emergencies."

"Agreed." Cody nodded. "Maybe in an ice cube in the freezer so I'm not too tempted to unlock myself."

"From what I've heard, you'll need to start slowly with how long you wear it. I wouldn't want you stuck in it and in true pain while I'm out on a shift or something." I glanced at the cage again. "This is fucking hot as hell, and I can't wait to see it on you."

Cody's eyes shone and he smiled. "*That's* what I've been waiting to hear." He stood up, and shucked his pants and briefs. "So, I've been reading up and it says I'll have to keep it lubed so I don't get rubbed raw." Cody reached for the bag and produced a small tube of lubrication.

Smearing his cock with lube, fitting the ring and cage over him, and locking him safe and sound inside was one of the most highly erotic moments of my life. And on top of that, trying to do it all without stimulating that gorgeous dick was the hardest thing I'd ever done. But once Cody was caged and locked, I took a step back to look at him and lost my breath.

"Fuck, that's beautiful." I reached for him, running my hands along his hips and stomach. "And it's *all* mine."

Cody smiled and pulled his pants back up. "Whoa, that's going to take some getting used to." He wiggled and shifted until the cage fit better into his jeans. Cody produced a chain from his pocket. "You want the key on a ring or on a chain?"

I thought momentarily. "Chain." I liked the idea of having the key around my neck.

Cody slipped the key onto the chain and then reached his arms around my neck to fasten the clasp. Our chests met and our eyes locked. "I guess I belong to you now," Cody's words were breathy.

"And I belong to you," I whispered before leaning in to capture his lips with mine for a brief kiss. "If at any time it's too much or you don't find any pleasure in it, you've got to be open with me."

Cody nibbled my bottom lip. "Baby, seeing how turned on *you* are is pleasure enough. But, I promise, if it's ever not enjoyable or I'm not into it anymore, I'll let you know. Same thing for you though. Holding a key is pretty huge. If you ever want out, all you have to do is say the word." He kissed me again. "Agreed?"

"Agreed." I kissed him. "How does it feel?" I cupped Cody's resin covered bulge.

"The more it's on, the softer it gets."

"Your body is heating the material." I rubbed him and shivered at the thought of his cock all locked up and belonging to me.

"Probably take it off when I sleep for a while. The guy at Leather Sunday said hard-ons overnight can cause discomfort and rub raw spots until I'm used to it."

"Oh!" I remembered something I'd heard once. "You'll have to sit to pee if you've got it on."

Cody's eyes widened as he seemed to replay my words. "Yeah, I can definitely see how standing to pee would be awkward with the cage."

I maneuvered Cody so he was facing the large wall mirror in the small train car room. From behind him, his back plastered to my front, I wrapped my arms around him and ran them up and down his torso. Tracing the shell of his ear with my tongue, I whispered, "Every time that gorgeous cock starts to get hard, I want you to think of me. Every time you want to caress your balls and jack yourself, think of me. Next time we have time to ourselves, I'm going to rim your beautiful ass, lick your balls, spank you until your skin is throbbing and pink, and tease your nipples until you want to cry. And the whole time, your dick will be begging, aching, straining against the cage. But, you won't be able to come until I allow it."

Cody whimpered and reached up and around my neck. "Promise me you won't let me come until you've fucked my face so hard I'm gasping for breath and trying not to gag on your cock."

"Since you're the one locked up, you don't get to beg for such things, but fucking your face is definitely not a hardship, so I'm thinking it can be worked out." I grazed my nails over Cody's pecs, meeting his gaze in the mirror when his nipples pebbled tightly under my touch.

"We don't have to leave right away." Cody panted. "We can stay until check out time."

"No can do. We planned to help Jay finish the final touches on the Blue Jay. He'll be a hot mess with the opening so soon." I spun Cody around, pressed him to the desk until he was forced to sit with his legs wide open. "But, I love knowing I can get you so worked up. All hot and bothered." I nuzzled his neck, up to his jaw, and whispered softly in his ear. "How badly do you want to come right now?"

Cody groaned.

"How badly do you want me to take you over my knee and spank you until you're begging me to stop?"

"God, Kennedy, stop." Cody threw his head back, breathing deeply.

"How much do you want my tongue, my fingers, my cock buried in your perfect ass?" I tormented.

When Cody shivered and reached to cup himself, I knocked away his hand. "Uh-uh, no touching." I kissed him soundly. "No worries, baby. I'll make sure we get some time together very soon."

"Promise?"

"Sure as shit, I promise." I held his face in my hands. "Because as badly as you want all of those things? I want them just as badly."

Twenty minutes later, I'd checked out of the hotel.

Cody situated himself in the driver's seat then sent a sexy scowl my way.

"What?" I couldn't help but chuckle.

"At least I won't get sleepy. My cock is throbbing, and these jeans are way too tight for this damn cage," Cody groused.

"You can take it off if it's too much," I began.

"Hell no, I'm not giving in that soon. I'll be fine."

I smiled because I knew Cody wouldn't back down from a challenge.

Three hours later, we pulled into BJ and found a crowd of people gathered on the town square.

"What the hell?" Cody muttered.

"Shit, look who's right in the middle of it." I pointed.

"Vicki Stringer. Why am I not surprised?" Cody growled.

We parked and climbed out. I smirked slightly when I saw Cody adjusting himself as covertly as possible.

"Those, those, *men* have already brought disgrace to this town." Vicki Stringer stood on a bench screaming at the top of her lungs. "Evil. Evil is what they are and evil is what they are spreading. Their types are only capable of sin and debauchery. Look what they've done with your restaurant. Turned it into a cesspool of pornography. And you're allowing those monsters to influence your children with that center of sexual sin? Do you know what men like them, homosexuals, do with children?"

I glanced around and saw that Jay wasn't around. *Thank goodness.*

Levi stood at the edge of the crowd with his jaw clenched and his arms crossed.

I didn't see Micah or Cole.

Just as I approached Ms. Stringer, I stopped as my Captain sauntered up. "I got this Marks. Go on home." His words were pleasant, but I recognized the tone as an order that allowed no room for argument.

As Captain worked to quiet Vicki, my fellow officers worked to disperse the crowd.

"Well, that was a shit show." I breathed deeply as Cody and Levi came to stand by my side.

"Thoughts on how to handle this?" Cody ran a hand through his hair.

"I could kill her and dump her down the backside of Blueridge Hill," Levi growled through gritted teeth.

"God, Levi, don't say stuff like that around me. I'm a police officer, I have to take things like that seriously." I elbowed him. "She's not worth it."

"I swear to God, if she ruins what that kid has worked so hard for…" Levi's words bubbled with emotion.

"She won't ruin it." Cody shook his head. "Let's give Micah and Cole the whole run down, but we'll tell Jay just enough to let him know there was an issue. Don't upset him."

"Fine, but then what?" Levi demanded.

"I think we convince Jay we should have an open house at the Blue Jay. Invite all the people who plan to volunteer their time or services. Then let people speak about the great things we have planned and how it will help kids." Cody nodded as he spoke, the plan obviously coming to life more and more in his head. "We have more voices, a better plan, and a history in this town to support us. Stringer has nothing but wild accusations, homophobia, and not even a year of living here. We stand together and take her down."

The three of us headed to the Blue Jay to finish up final touches and plan the open house.

CHAPTER 19

CODY

"Oh my god, it's like the BJ boys are sharing a brain." Jay did a little victory dance. "I've been thinking of doing an open house. This is perfect."

Levi held Jay's hands. "The main thing, aside from letting the community see the place and get the kids excited about coming here, is to give the volunteers and sponsors a chance to explain why it's going to be such a great place for kids."

"Yeah, that sounds great." Jay cocked his head to the side. "Why do you seem so serious?"

"I think Levi's just a little worried about that Stringer lady." I piped up. "She's been causing a stink over Leather Sundays and even wants the B & B closed. She's a wild card."

Kennedy nodded. "Yeah, Captain says she's been a regular thorn in his side since she came to town."

"Well, bitch can leave. Buh-bye!" Jay waved dramatically. "Don't let the door hit you on the way out."

"Either way, let's make the open house spectacular, okay?" Levi pulled Jay close and walked with him down the hallway.

"What did you leave out?" Micah asked.

Kennedy and I glanced at each other.

"Spill it," Micah urged with Cole right by his side.

"Stringer had a big crowd at the town square when we pulled into town this morning." Kennedy started.

"Oh yeah, that's right, so…how was Indy?" Cole asked.

Kennedy blushed.

I couldn't help but smile. The chastity device felt tight when I let my mind wander back to our time in the city.

"Well, if it's *that* good then we better head north and soon." Micah laughed and elbowed Cole. "But, what about Stringer?"

I curled my lip. "We drove up to find her standing on a bench, screaming about the evils of *our type,* and our bad influence on the youth. Sin, pornography, debauchery. Apparently, we are responsible for it all."

Cole frowned "Should we let Jay know a little more detail so he's not taken off guard at the open house? I'm sure she'll try to cause trouble."

"Actually, I think we should keep it to ourselves between now and the open house, but let him know right before opening so he's not shook up if she starts shit." I knew Jay would pretend not to be fazed, but if he knew of Vicki's machinations now, they would bother him. The less time he had to worry about it, the better. "Can we make sure some of the police department is present during the open house?" I asked Kennedy.

"Sure." Kennedy agreed. "A lot of them will probably come anyway because we all plan on doing volunteer hours. We'll speak on behalf of the department regarding our plans and continued support."

We spent the rest of the day securing the date, time, and attendees for the open house along with spreading the word on social media. Cole and Micah set out with flyers to hang in surrounding communities while Cody and I hit the streets of Blueridge to spread the word.

In five days, we would invite the masses to visit the Blue Jay and hopefully win them over.

I didn't see Kennedy for the next five days due to work and life just getting in the way. So when I snuck up behind him in the walk-in pantry at the Blue Jay an hour before the open house, I was pleased and not at all surprised to find myself spun around and thrown against the closed door.

Kennedy held my hips tight and nuzzled my neck. "Mmmm, I don't know whether to kick your ass for sneaking up on me, or kiss you senseless because I've missed you so much."

I pressed my hips against his and moved so my neck was more exposed to his teasing kisses. "How 'bout you do both?"

"Perfect plan," Kennedy whispered before kissing me, tracing my lips with his tongue, nipping and soothing the sting. "Tonight? After the open house?"

I nodded.

Kennedy reached down to cup my dick. "Oh fuck, you've got the cage on?" His knee shoved hard between my legs.

"I've had it off and on as I get used to it." I rolled my hips to press my bulge into his palm. "Thought it might make you happy to know I was wearing it tonight."

"I love it," Kennedy growled before moving his kisses along my jawline and devouring my neck. "I love that you have it on. I love that you wore it for me." He brought up his hands to frame my face. "I love *you*."

His words caught my heart and wrapped it in soft warmth and steely desire. "I love you, too."

A knock at the pantry door broke our private paradise. "Stop fucking in the pantry. We've got to prove to the community we aren't a bad influence."

Based on the voice, I knew Levi likely stood right outside the door with his broad shoulders squared and both arms crossed over his chest.

"Tonight?" I bit my lip and waited for Kennedy's answer.

"No way in hell I'd miss it."

When we emerged from the pantry, Levi rolled his eyes. "Created a damn monster with those two," he grumbled at Jay as the younger man walked up.

"Come on. Let's make sure we have the order of the night perfected." Jay ignored Levi, winked at

Kennedy and I, and snapped his fingers to get Micah and Cole's attention.

"Did he just snap at me?" Cole feigned disbelief.

"Yes, yes he did." Micah deadpanned.

"Come *on*. We've got things to do." Jay stomped his foot. "This is the big night, almost even bigger than opening day. Tonight is our one chance to wow the community and get the kids interested in coming."

"Babe, one thing we have to prepare for is that the kids may not come in droves in the beginning. Think about how scared you would have been to show up at a place like the BJ." Levi rubbed Jay's shoulders.

Jay nodded. "I would have been scared, but I think if we make it look cool and welcoming and entice them with games and food, we can get them a lot easier."

Kennedy cleared his throat. "So, Captain Scott wanted to make sure we're all aware that Stringer is still stirring shit about the B & B's Leather Sundays and about the Blue Jay opening." Kennedy glanced at all of us as if looking for permission to tell Jay more. He must have gotten the answer he was looking for because he continued. "Stringer's been spewing a lot of hatred and rumors about us and the BJ."

Jay gasped. "Like what?" he demanded indignantly.

Micah rolled his eyes "Like we're only in this to corrupt and recruit the teens to our evil sinful way of life. You know, the usual."

"Oh no she didn't," Jay quipped. "Hell, no. She's not going to ruin this."

"We won't let her, babe." Levi pulled Jay close. "But, we all need to know what she's about. Be prepared for her hatred. Stand tall and firm. Don't let her get to us."

"Boys, I'm a performer at heart." Jay popped an elbow on a cocked hip. "We're going to have a packed house hanging on our every word, eating out of our hands, and we'll steal the show, leaving Vicki Stringer in the proverbial dust." He snapped the fingers of his other hand in a wild gesture. "We've got this, bitches."

"Oh lord, he's getting sassy." Levi laughed. "He means business."

"Let's go get 'em then," I said.

As I walked to the large open gathering area, I glanced around the Blue Jay. I was proud of what Jay had built, of what we'd helped him create. I wasn't ready to let one hateful woman tear us down.

At exactly six o'clock, we opened the doors and allowed the large crowd to wander in.

Jay welcomed the visitors. "Feel free to take self tours, ask questions, and grab some snacks. We'll gather back here at six-thirty for a little discussion session." Jay swung his arms wide to indicate the center was open for exploring.

Thirty minutes later, Vicki Stringer sat front and center in the gathering room looking like she'd swallowed a lemon and had a corncob shoved up her ass.

Officers, on and off duty, lined the walls and a few sat around her.

My heart surged as Jay stood at the front of the group.

"Thank you all for being here tonight." Jay smiled and turned into the magical performer we all knew him to be. "I didn't have a place like the Blue Jay when I was growing up. God, how I wish I'd had somewhere to get food, stay warm, talk to friends, and get some help with homework. In one week, The Blue Jay will open, and we will welcome every single individual who comes through our doors with open arms." Jay turned to look at the row of people who were lined up to speak on behalf of the BJ. "And we've got *a lot* of assistance to offer. I'll turn the floor over to the wonderful people of this community, and surrounding towns, who have committed their time and services to make the Blue Jay a success. With everyone's support, we'll reach kids right when they feel the most lost and alone." Jay waved forward the first speaker.

With Micah's mom, Kennedy's adoptive parents, and my father at her side, my mom started, "On behalf of this whole little group of grateful parents, I want to say how proud we are of what our sons have done. Some of the boys were lucky enough to have support growing up, some of them were not." Her voice caught on emotion. "If the Blue Jay can give just *one* lost child a place to feel welcome and at home, save the life of just *one* young person, then it's worth every single bit of blood, sweat, and tears that went into building and organizing it." Mom took a deep breath and smiled through her tears. "No child will ever feel unloved, unsupported, or unappreciated here. Hatred has no place inside these walls. If I do anything with the rest of my life, I will be damn sure that every kid who walks through those doors knows they are perfect just the way they are."

Once she'd finished, Mom's little posse hugged her close as the crowd clapped.

Jay stood beside Levi and wept silently, obviously overcome with love and appreciation for her words.

Kennedy's parents came to stand by him, a show of solidarity.

Next, three school counselors and five teachers took turns voicing the importance of having support outside of the school setting. "I know I speak for each of us, and for all the teachers who couldn't be here tonight, I see a place like the Blue Jay being a lifesaver for many students."

Matt Stringer, Vicki's son, emerged from the side of the room. "I wasn't sure I would speak here tonight." He glanced at his mother in the front row. "But, I can't stand by quietly. The Blue Jay is exactly the type of place *any* kid would love to have in times of trouble or loneliness. I know if I'd had this place when I felt hated at home, I would have counted it as a blessing. I plan on helping here as much as I can."

Vicki's eyes narrowed and her lip curled in disgust at her son's words even though they weren't specifically aimed at her.

I quickly realized that each person who spoke to the crowd had a less-than-subtle message for Stringer hidden within with their supportive and informative message to the community. Stringer face got redder and her fists clenched tighter with each and every show of support.

I watched her closely.

"She's clean," Kennedy whispered beside me. "She got an accidental pat down before she came in."

I turned a questioning look to him.

"Let's just say two of my fellow officers were terribly clumsy. Poor Ms. Stringer got jostled a bit and her bag fell to the ground." Kennedy coughed to cover his laugh. "But no weapons on her."

I gritted my teeth to keep from laughing out loud. "Dang clumsy oafs."

"Right?" Kennedy nodded, his face serious but his eyes dancing.

Levi stepped to the front. "My family has been a part of this town since our founding fathers settled on Blueridge. Wells, Edwards, and Parker are names synonymous with honesty, respect, and integrity. Any of you who have been here a long time or done business with any of us knows that to be true. The Blue Jay was built with love and will soon become an integral part of Blueridge Junction. The folk in this town know good hearts and good intentions when they see them, and I'm trusting to you recognize that now." Levi glanced around the room. "Every single person here is an individual, unique, and special. And Blueridge has always been a place where a person could be true to themselves. Don't allow an outsider to spread hate and divide a town that has stood strong for generations." Levi paused and stared right at Vicki. "Now, *some* of you may want to take your leave. For those who'd like to stay and visit, please feel free to eat more snacks and continue your tours of the Blue Jay. I, for one, am looking forward to seeing a lot of attendees when we open next week. Young people, tell your friends. Bring as many as you'd like. The more the merrier."

The crowd clapped and whistled before standing and slowly beginning to mill about and disperse.

"I think it's time you go, ma'am." I took my place beside Levi and addressed Stringer.

Gaping at us like a fish out of water, Stringer finally stood. Glaring at us for several moments as if trying to find the words she wanted to say, Vicki eventually growled and turned to storm out the door.

Kennedy, Levi, and I followed her, and I knew several other officers were right behind us.

"Ms. Stringer, may I have a word?" Kennedy spoke up.

I almost gave myself whiplash turning to see what the hell he was up to. He shook his head as if to hush me. *Well, all right then.*

Stringer turned and barged right up to Kennedy. "You should be ashamed of yourself. All of you should be," she pointed to the other officers.

"Officers of the law allowing and *supporting* such sin and evil. You mark my words, all of those gay men working with teens is trouble waiting to happen. The devil's work is taking place here."

"Ms. Stringer, did you see that show of support in there?" Kennedy gestured back to the building. "That's not the devil's work. That's called love and support and positive relationships. Do you really want to take on all of that? You have no proof of anything bad happening. I'm an officer of the law. Cole is a teacher. Most of the other guys have lived their entire lives in this town without one iota of accusation against them. Stop fighting so hard to hate your son and just love him. He's not a sin, he's not evil, and he's not something to be ashamed of. He's your *son*."

Vicki opened her mouth to argue, but Kennedy held up his hand, palm outward.

"You're welcome to stay in Blueridge. No one will stop you from living here." Kennedy crossed both arms over his chest. "But it would be a lot more enjoyable and peaceful for everyone involved if you'd stop trying to ruin our little town and work on your own happiness."

"I'll be damned if I'll stay in a town like this. You're all going to burn in hell one day. I won't let the likes of these savages pull me into their sins." Vicki spewed spittle as she raged on.

"So be it," Kennedy answered softly.

"Allow me to help you to your car, ma'am." The police captain stepped forward. "When you're ready to leave town, please do contact the department. We'd be honored to offer you an escort. For your own safety of course."

The group of officers and our crew had to turn around and head back inside before our guffaws overtook the night.

Kennedy stood by my side. "Well, that went very well. Don't you think?"

"Very well indeed." I gazed around the Blue Jay. "I think we'll be overflowing with teens come next week."

"Who wouldn't want to spend their time here?" Kennedy smirked. "It's pretty kick ass."

"Agreed." I nodded. "Speaking of kick ass. Didn't you promise to beat my ass when the open house was over?" *Officer* Kennedy putting Vicki in her place had me all hot and bothered.

"Doesn't look like it's over," Kennedy pondered.

"It's over enough. They'll never miss us." I nudged his arm. "Come on."

"Okay, but ride with me. I need to run by Levi's before we hit your place."

Ten minutes later, I wandered into Levi's kitchen, as much at home there as I was in my own place. "You 'bout done?" I hollered down the stairs at Kennedy. Impatient was an understatement for how I was feeling at the moment.

"I can't find what I'm looking for." Kennedy hollered. "Come help me look."

"Good lord, man. Do you *have* to find it right now?" I grumbled as I headed down the basement steps.

"Lock the door," Kennedy demanded from the base of the stairs.

His command caused me to freeze momentarily.

Then I saw why.

His completely naked body adorned in only a leather jock and harness punched me in the gut and had me hastily locking the door.

Kennedy followed me to the middle of the basement. He stood close behind me, but didn't touch any part of me. My body was on fire, my knees trembled, and my heart pounded. I gazed around the basement in absolute shock and extreme anticipation.

Leather whips, nipple clamps, a ball gag, a cock ring, leather bindings, and a flogger were spread out on the bed. A sling hung from the ceiling beam and called to me, teasing my balls with its very presence. "Holy fuck," I breathed out.

"You like?" Kennedy whispered in my ear. "I've been busy setting up our own little sex dungeon. Levi and Jay are going to stay at your place. I thought maybe bringing it back to where we got our start would make it even better."

"Holy fuck," I repeated.

"You're mine. Down here, I own you. You got that?" Kennedy finally stepped in, pulled me to his chest, and cupped my cock. "This is mine, your orgasms are mine, and your ass is mine. Your safe word is Indy. You got that?"

I wrapped my arms behind his head and whimpered as I sank back against his body.

"Say it, Cody. Say, 'you own me. I'm yours, body and soul. The safe word is Indy.'"

Kennedy's command shook me to the core. "You own me. I'm yours, body and soul." I panted. "The safe word is Indy."

"Very good." Kennedy stepped away. "Now, get naked. I have plans for that gorgeous body of yours."

We spent the next twenty-four hours exploring our newfound roles, breaking in the sling, christening all the toys, and earning our way deeper into the kink and play of leather. My safe word was never used. And I found an extreme appreciation for that damn basement.

BJ Boys Series Epilogue

"A toast!" Jay raised his glass and waited for everyone in the room to do the same. "I just want to take a moment," he paused for dramatic effect, but it was clear he was also attempting to gather his emotions. "A moment to express just how happy I am to have all of the BJ Boys together as it was meant to be. We are truly a family and blessed to have each other."

Glasses were clinked and *cheers* murmured.

"And now," Jay drew out his words, "I have a grand announcement." He paused again. "Levi and I have decided to grow our little family." He reached behind the couch and retrieved a wiggly ball of wrinkles and fur. The bulldog puppy squirmed and licked at Jay's face. "BJ Boys, meet Brutus."

After several moments of ohhhs and ahhhs, Micah cleared his throat and pulled Cole close to his side. "We kinda have an announcement to make, as well."

Cole blushed and his eyes filled with tears. "We're adopting. The baby is due in a month."

Tears and congratulations flowed and hugs were given all around.

"Oh my god, this night just keeps getting better," Jay gushed.

At that moment, Cody dropped to his knee in front of Kennedy and the entire room went silent except for the slight snorts coming from Brutus.

"Kennedy, I never thought I could love you more than I hated you. But I was wrong. I used to think you and I were bound to fight and would never get past that. Turns out we were bound to fall in love; we just needed an extra push. Our love isn't perfect, probably never will be, but it's perfect *for us*. I love every part of you, and I want to spend the rest of my life with you." Cody pulled a ring from his pocket. "Will you marry me?"

A teary-eyed and laughing Kennedy said yes and the room erupted in cheers.

"Why are you all pouty," Levi asked Jay as the commotion calmed.

"I want a wedding and a baby and all I got is this adorable puppy." Jay stuck out his bottom lip.

"You're enough of a baby for me to take care of...for now." Levi kissed the side of Jay's head. "Plus, I'm sure Cody and Kennedy will let you help with the planning of their wedding until it's time to plan ours."

Jay turned a beaming smile to Levi. "Daddy, did you just admit to wanting to marry me some day?"

Levi smiled and pulled Jay in for a kiss. "Yeah, I think I just did."

The BJ Boys spent the rest of the weekend celebrating love, friendship, and family.

FROM THE AUTHOR

NOTE- The stories about the haunted happenings in Indianapolis were gathered from a haunted tour I went on this summer at GenCon.

Some books about haunted Indiana:

http://amzn.to/2piCr9g

http://amzn.to/2piVtvZ

The train car rooms at Union Station are real. I haven't stayed in one, but I've seen the rooms. So cool! The only thing that would keep me from staying in the one is the above mentioned haunted tales!

Don't miss my other male/male romance books in the Something About Him series! author.to/ADEllisAmazon

THANK YOU FOR READING! I hope you enjoyed; please take a moment to leave a review. If you're reading on a file/device that doesn't take you to a review option, please consider finding the book on the platform of your choice and giving a star rating and a short review. It doesn't have to be long and drawn out, just a few sentences about how it made you feel, what you liked/didn't like. THANK YOU!!

If you are interested in my male/female contemporary romance series (Torey Hope) or my other male/male romance books, please check out my website to find information about all of my books. Or, search your favorite book platform for my name and see if something tickles your fancy.

A.D. Ellis

ABOUT THE AUTHOR

A.D. Ellis is an Indiana girl, born and raised. She spends much of her time in central Indiana teaching alternative education in the inner city of Indianapolis, being a mom to two amazing school-aged children, and laughing at a precocious cat. A lot of her time is also devoted to phone call avoidance and her hatred of cooking.

She loves chocolate, wine, pizza, and naps along with reading and writing romance. These loves don't leave much time for housework, much to the chagrin of her husband of nearly two decades. Who would pick cleaning the house over a nap or a good book? She uses any extra time to increase her fluency in sarcasm.

FREE books-- sign up at bit.ly/ADEllisNews for a FREE male/female romance. Sign up at http://www.subscribepage.com/ADEllisNewsMMR omance for a FREE male/male romance book.

Facebook www.facebook.com/adellisauthor

Twitter www.twitter.com/ADEllisAuthor

Website http://adellisauthor.com/

ACKNOWLEDGEMENTS

This is always one of the hardest parts of finishing a book, but quite possibly the most important part! It's so hard because I fear I'll miss someone who has helped me out, supported me, been a listening ear, or offered advice and encouragement. If I miss listing your name here, please know it wasn't on purpose, and I love you dearly!

A dear friend once again made this book possible. I'm not sure he understands how much his input means to me and how he shapes my stories with his words, answers, experiences, and heart. Thank you, Brett, as always. Don't ever doubt your potential and how lucky people are to know you.

And, to Gage. You are truly an amazing person. Thank you, again, for all of your help and input. Not to get all mushy, but you have an incredible future ahead of you because you can do absolutely anything you set your mind to. I feel blessed to get to watch you reach the stars.

To Kurt and Chris- thanks so much for answering the frantic questions I'd throw your way at the oddest hours. PRIDE in Indianapolis 2017, Kurt's question of "Have you ever thought of writing a story about someone in the leather community?" THIS is what happens when a question piques an author's curiosity. Thank you both for your help.

To my friend, fellow author, and cover designer, Kay Simone at <u>Kay Simone Creative</u>. Thank you for listening to my vision and making it beautiful! You are a superb talent and I'm lucky to call you my designer.

To my dear beta readers. Your input, feedback, and encouragement has proven invaluable to me! I truly trust you all and value your opinions more than you'll probably ever understand. Thank you to my newest betas as well. When I needed fresh new eyes who had never read any of these characters you were there for me and helped me so much!

To my Ellis Elite Private Discussion Group— THANK YOU! Those of you who list me in contests and comments and shout outs all the time, you're amazing and I love you for always working to get my name out there! If I start naming people here, I'll be sure to miss some; just know if you've ever shared my name or my books, it means the world to me and I appreciate you more than you'll ever know!

To my READERS!! You are what keeps me going. You are the reason I write some days. When I don't feel like I have it in me, I'll get a message or comment from a reader about how a story of mine has touched them, and *that* will be the inspiration and motivation for me to write. As long as these stories are in my head, I'll keep sharing them with you.

To the BLOGGERS who read and review and share my books!! You are beyond a shadow of a doubt some of the most dedicated and selfless people I've ever known! Thank you so much for being such a support to those of us who have stories to tell. I love BLOGGERS!

To my Juice Box ladies! Thank you so much for welcoming me into your crew and sharing your knowledge, experience, advice, and fun with me! Having some real-life authors/friends I can collaborate with is a great feeling. Dance parties, lunches, movies, videos, wine, painting, pizza, sushi, cookies...the list goes on and on! Thank you for letting me be a Juice Boxer!

Cheryl Brooks- the blurb queen. That is all.

To my fellow authors. Those of you who read my work, share your work with me, cross-promote with me, and offer advice and support, THANK YOU! You make this a little easier and enjoyable.

To my family and friends. I know most of you don't understand my obsession with getting these stories out of my head and on paper, but you're proud of me either way. Some of you get to read my books, some of you get to see cover ideas, some of you have to watch me lose myself in a story, some of you have to hear me vent about the hard parts of all of this; all of you love me and support me and for that, I am truly lucky and grateful.

CONNECT WITH A.D. ELLIS

Follow my website http://www.adellisauthor.com or find me on Facebook

http://www.facebook.com/adellisauthor

If you want updates about releases, interviews, sales, giveaways, and more please sign up for my newsletter bit.ly/ADEllisNews

You can also find me on Twitter http://www.twitter.com/ADEllisAuthor

Find me on Spotify if you'd like to listen to my playlists (mainly the songs I listened to while writing). Just search for A.D. Ellis.

www.ingramcontent.com/pod-product-compliance
Lightning Source LLC
Chambersburg PA
CBHW020419030726
47495CB00006B/1576